PREP

The toughest hoods in Manhattan's prep schools aren't like other street thugs. They aren't poor and angry—they're just angry. They aren't outsiders; none of them have spent their lives trying to make it out of anywhere. They go to the best schools and spend their summers in the Hamptons.

Prep-school hoods try to dress just like hoods from Harlem and Brooklyn, except their clothing is always brand-new designer-label. Their chinos are usually a size too big, so that they hang loosely at the hips and bunch up around their Timberland boots, and bright Tag Heuers are on all their wrists. They normally wear a Tommy Hilfiger or Polo shirt with a nice-size label, and a North Face jacket, hood and all. Some of them even sport crest rings. They're kind of funny to watch, until they decide to put somebody in the hospital.

OTHER SPEAK BOOKS

PREP

PREP

Jake
Coburn

speak
An Imprint of Penguin Group (USA) Inc.

Special thanks to Elaine Markson Literary Agency

SPEAK
Published by the Penguin Group
Penguin Group (USA) Inc., 345 Hudson Street, New York, New York 10014, U.S.A.
Penguin Group (Canada), 10 Alcorn Avenue, Toronto, Ontario, Canada M4V 3B2
(a division of Pearson Penguin Canada Inc.)
Penguin Books Ltd, 80 Strand, London WC2R 0RL, England
Penguin Ireland, 25 St Stephen's Green, Dublin 2, Ireland (a division of Penguin Books Ltd)
Penguin Group (Australia), 250 Camberwell Road, Camberwell, Victoria 3124, Australia
(a division of Pearson Australia Group Pty Ltd)
Penguin Books India Pvt Ltd, 11 Community Centre,
Panchsheel Park, New Delhi - 110 017, India
Penguin Group (NZ), Cnr Airborne and Rosedale Roads, Albany,
Auckland, New Zealand (a division of Pearson New Zealand Ltd)
Penguin Books (South Africa) (Pty) Ltd, 24 Sturdee Avenue,
Rosebank, Johannesburg 2196, South Africa

Registered Offices: Penguin Books Ltd, 80 Strand, London WC2R 0RL, England

Published in the United States of America by Dutton Books,
a member of Penguin Group (USA) Inc., 2003
Published by Speak, an imprint of Penguin Group (USA) Inc., 2005

1 3 5 7 9 10 8 6 4 2

THE LIBRARY OF CONGRESS HAS CATALOGED THE DUTTON EDITION AS FOLLOWS:
Coburn, Jake.
Prep / Jake Coburn.—1st ed.
p. cm.
Summary: A one-time tag artist, Nick tries to come to terms with the death of a friend,
to protect the brother of his would-be girlfriend, to escape the violence of wealthy
New York City prep-school hoods, and to figure out who he really is.
ISBN 0-525-47135-9
[1. Interpersonal relations—Fiction. 2. Gangs—Fiction.
3. Self-perception—Fiction. 4. New York (N.Y.)—Fiction.] I. Title.
PZ7.C6365Pr 2003 [Fic]—dc21 2003048322

Speak ISBN 0-14-240307-5

Designed by Heather Wood

Printed in the United States of America

PREP

New York City

not so long ago...

Friday Night

The streets were empty but I didn't mind. A little after four in the morning, Manhattan settles quietly into a cool dawn. As I jogged across 92nd Street, looking for a pay phone, all I heard was the occasional clicking of traffic lights and the steady breathing of steaming manholes. Birds don't sing on Broadway.

The night had been a bust from the start. I was supposed to meet Victoria at Bella Luna at eight, but by eight-thirty I was nursing my second beer. There were two girls in a booth near my table and, waiting there with a pair of menus in front of me, I felt like they both knew I was getting stood up. I probably should've bailed, but I hadn't gone out on a date in a while and I was tired of being alone.

Victoria and I had been set up on a blind date by our matchmaking math tutor, Rachel Line, and I was beginning to worry that I wouldn't recognize her. I knew Victoria was a senior at Dwiggins and a brunette, but I'd daydreamed the rest. All week, I'd been imagining fragile green eyes and a long, doorstep kiss good night.

At a quarter to nine, a girl in a navy pea coat walked into Bella Luna. She scanned the tables and picked me out of the lineup with an apologetic wave.

"I'm so, so sorry," she said, slipping out of her jacket and sitting down at our table. Victoria was wearing a cashmere turtleneck and a serious pair of heels, and sitting there in jeans, I couldn't decide if I was underdressed or she was overdressed. "I'm doing this internship at a lab and I couldn't get away." She had warm almond eyes and a stunning figure that made me swallow.

"No problem. What sort of work were you doing?" Without thinking, I reached for my water glass. I wasn't thirsty. In fact, I had to go to the bathroom.

"Biology," she said, adjusting her silverware so that the knife and fork were equally spaced from the plate. "But it's really more like bio slash chem. We're studying the effect of these new seizure medications on hamsters." Victoria lifted her pointer finger and hailed the nearest waiter. "Can I get a Diet Coke with two pieces of lemon?"

"I hear your father's a director," I began. Rachel had mentioned that Victoria's father was a documentary filmmaker, and I'd decided that was a sign. I'd spent an entire study hall making a laundry list of directors for us to discuss. "What sort of stuff does he do?"

"Mostly political topics, like civil rights and abortion."

"It's got to be pretty cool to hear about different projects and shoots."

"I guess. But it's more my younger sister's thing than mine. I haven't seen the last couple."

"You feel like splitting a bottle of wine?" I said, trying to loosen up the evening.

Victoria laughed and shook her head disapprovingly. "What kind of a girl drinks half a bottle of wine for dinner?" I could name one, but I didn't answer. I was starting to get that student-government vibe. Maybe just a lot of extracurriculars.

The waiter walked back over with Victoria's soda, and she ordered the salmon with mashed potatoes on the side. I picked the pasta special and asked for another beer. After a pair of heavy pauses, I asked a few more questions about her father's documentaries. She didn't even know if he shot on video or film—I couldn't believe it. On the walk to Bella Luna, I'd scripted the entire evening so perfectly. Now I felt cheated.

After dinner, we window-shopped on Madison and then caught a midnight show of *A Streetcar Named Desire*. It's an old Brando film that I've watched dozens of times, and I figured Victoria would appreciate a Hollywood classic. But in the cab back to her apartment, she kept arguing that Stella should have left Stanley ten minutes into the movie. What can you say to that?

We got to Victoria's building around three. Her parents were in Connecticut for the weekend, so she and her sister had the place to themselves. Victoria kicked her heels into the living room, and I followed her down a short hallway.

She tapped lightly on a door. "I'm home," she said, twisting the glass knob.

"'Night, Vic," her sister mumbled. "'Night, Steve."

I looked at Victoria. I'd been called a lot of different nicknames, but never Steve.

Victoria wrapped her fingers around my wrist. "He's a guy that I *was* seeing."

"You sure?"

"Positive," she said and led me into the living room. "Completely positive."

She flicked on an oldies radio station and I walked toward the sliding glass doors leading out to the balcony. Across the river, New Jersey was spotted with distant lights, and from inside her apartment they looked like the tiny embers from a stamped-out fire.

I could see Victoria's reflection in the glass as she walked up behind me. She asked me to dance and I wrapped my arms around her waist. Before I could remember the name of the song, she was resting her cheek softly on my collar. I closed my eyes and listened to her gently exhale.

Halfway through Otis Redding's "Pain in My Heart," we started to kiss. Victoria rested her palms on my chest and let out a moan. I opened my eyes—I froze. I couldn't do this. She looked up at me with this confused expression, but I didn't know what to say. I didn't even like this girl.

All I wanted was to see Kris.

"This isn't right," I said, stepping away from her.

"What?"

"We're rushing it."

She stared up at me. "What do——"

"I can't explain it." I was furious at myself for leading her on, for leading myself on. "It's not you."

"I'm not asking for marriage," she said, sexily tilting her head.

"I'm really sorry. I just gotta go."

I felt like such an asshole leaving, but I knew I had to. I grabbed my jacket off the floor and left her standing there in the middle of her living room. Downstairs, the doorman opened the cast-iron door for me and I faded out into New York.

Now I was staking out a pay phone, trying to figure out what to say to Kris. You can't just call a girl up at four in the morning and tell her that you love her.

———

I saw Kris for the first time about a year ago. She was sitting at the counter of the Three Brothers diner on 82nd, a Lucky Strike dangling from her mouth, writing on a paper napkin. Her long black hair rested on her shoulders, and her light blue eyes filled the room.

She had this wonderful rhythm where she'd write a sentence, take a long drag, and exhale while she read it over. Every few minutes she would grin and begin writing urgently. Then there were periods where she wouldn't move at all.

I spent nearly an hour at the diner trying to figure out a good opening line. Normally when I meet a girl, she's with a group of people, girlfriends on either side dressed in the same fashion, just in different shades. They need each other, and they're never by themselves. But Kris sat alone on that diner stool and made every stranger around her look like extras.

I wanted to be able to slide up next to her, but I didn't have the courage to make that sort of move. On the screen, guys are always walking up to beautiful girls and charming them accidentally. They bump heads or say the same thing and laugh, but I needed to plan or I'd make a fool of myself.

It was my first time at the diner and I asked my waiter if she came there often. He laughed. "Every night."

Kris's answering machine picked up after three rings. Her new message was a clip from an early Tom Waits song, that was all. I missed the soft inflections of her voice. I hung up the phone and checked my watch. Her townhouse was only about fifteen blocks away, so I started walking. She'd probably be asleep, but I thought I could wake her. At least I could try.

When I first met Kris at the diner, we were stuck at "friends." She was dating this twenty-one-year-old guitar player named Luke Booker, and Kris's lips would curl into a smile every time she mentioned his name. Luke had gone to college for a semester or two, but he'd dropped out to promote his first album, *Starboard*. Luke's acoustic LP was all about sailing and weather patterns and how tough it was being him. I'd hung out with him a half-dozen times, and Luke loved to talk at me like he was Bob Dylan.

For the first few months, I kept trying to show Kris how full of shit Luke was without actually coming out and saying it. But it was hopeless, not even a dent. A girl will believe almost anything if a guy puts it in a song, especially if he's a really good-looking guy. So, I guess I settled for a best friend. I mean, right from the beginning Kris and I could talk for hours about the most random stuff, from applesauce to Zen and back again, and we never got bored. The way I saw it, the time Kris and I spent together was better than any date I'd ever gone on. She knew me better than anybody else. I just never got to wake up next to her.

On 88th Street, I passed the flashing yellow sign of a pool hall. The fluorescent "l"s in the word "Billiards" were pool cues, and I could see a guy at the bar studying a carefully folded news-paper. I sort of felt like joining him for a drink, but at that moment Kris was the only thing.

Then about a month ago, Kris called and told me that Luke was going on a cross-country tour, that they'd broken up. I was standing in my bathroom, smoking a Lucky out the window, and I suddenly felt like falling to my knees and kissing the bath-mat. She said it was both their decisions, but for the next few weeks Kris was a wreck. When she wasn't crying, she was talk-ing about how she was so happy not to be in a "relationship." It drove me crazy. I understood that she needed to talk about Luke but I couldn't handle all the details. And every time I felt like she was finally starting to get past him, he'd write her a letter or leave some staged message on her answering machine that she'd play for me over and over again.

I stopped at a bodega on 85th and Broadway. The tile floor

squeaked as I walked in, and the soggy air smelled like overripe bananas. I ordered a large coffee, regular, and slipped a dollar bill out of my wallet.

I still couldn't believe I'd walked out on Victoria like that. For the last year I'd been able to go out on dates, I'd even had a couple drunken hookups, but Victoria was my first date since Kris and Luke split. And at some point during our kiss, I realized I was done pretending or ignoring or whatever—I was in love with Kris. I didn't have a clue what to say or do, but I knew that I had to be with her.

The woman behind the counter walked away to get a paper cup and I thought about reaching for a bag of M&M's. I hadn't swiped a pack since seventh grade, but I knew she wouldn't spot me. Even if she did, I'd just pay for them. The woman walked back toward me with my coffee, then turned around again to get the sugars. My right hand darted out and slid the small bag into my pants pocket. Before she came back, I pulled the M&M's out and tossed them onto the counter. I used to be able to grab two.

In junior high, we'd stage fights inside bodegas to distract the cashier. Four of us would roll in wearing our school blazers and sagging ties, and when the guys in front started roughing each other up, we'd trick-or-treat our way down the aisles. The fights never lasted more than a minute or two, but you can only fit so much in a backpack. We were such punks. We always had the money to pay.

By the time I reached Kris's place, I'd finished the coffee and half the candy. She lived in a white four-story townhouse with her mother and younger brother. When Kris was twelve, her father gave up his advertising job and skipped off to California to open a restaurant.

I tossed a few more M&M's in my mouth and held the next one carefully, like I was guessing the weight. I noticed my fingers were shaking. There'd been so many nights when I wanted to walk over to Kris's and wake her up, but I'd never had the nerve to actually do it.

I leaned back and threw the M&M at Kris's window.

———

I went back to Three Brothers the next night with the idea of asking Kris out. She didn't go to my high school, so I figured if everything went horribly, at least nobody but the two of us would know. A block before I reached the diner, I stopped at a bodega and bought a pack of her cigarettes, Lucky Strikes. It couldn't hurt.

I strolled into the diner with enough hubris to captain the Titanic. Just as I'd hoped, she was sitting at the end of the counter scribbling away. But this time, she was writing in a brown leather diary.

I walked smoothly up to the counter and sat down two stools away. Signaling to the waiter for a cup of coffee, I fumbled in my pocket for a cigarette and pretended to search for a lighter. With as much charm as I could muster, I asked if I could borrow hers.

Kris didn't even look up. Instead she just slid her lighter across the counter like a bartender and kept writing. As I went to light my cigarette, she suddenly stopped, turned toward me, nearly said something, and then turned back.

I walked down to her with my coffee in one hand and the lighter in the other. "Can I buy you a cup of coffee?"

She stopped writing again and rested her pen in the diary. "Do I have a choice?"

———

The M&M arced over Kris's third-story window and disappeared onto the rooftop. Fuck. I should have gotten peanut M&M's. They were heavier, but you didn't get as many in a bag.

I poured out two more and threw. The first one sliced to the left but the second bounced off the lower pane of Kris's window. The sound of the candy smacking against the glass echoed down the row of houses. I checked the block and leaned up against a Camry. If the M&M's didn't work, I could try and climb the ivy to her balcony.

Halfway through my next windup, I spotted Kris's younger brother, Danny, turning the corner. He strode loosely down the block, his legs swinging like a marionette's and his forty sloshing back and forth with each of his long strides. Danny was a freshman at a small prep school for kids with really high IQs. We'd only hung out together a couple times, but Kris loved to tell me stories about him.

I checked Kris's window again. No light. Nothing. When I turned back to Danny, he'd vanished. Walking out into the street, I scanned the block. Where the hell had he gone?

I emptied the bag of M&M's into my palm, ate a few, and then pitched the entire handful. Two or three of them shattered against Kris's window and splintered back down to the sidewalk.

"Nick?" Danny whispered.

I turned around. Danny was peeking out from behind a

couple of garbage cans up the block. "Man, am I glad to see you," he said.

"Why'd you hide?"

"I was just surveying," he said, smiling. "I wanted to make sure it was you." As Danny climbed over the wall of garbage cans, the forty seemed to throw off his balance, and he ended up knocking a trash can over. It crashed against the sidewalk, and he burst out laughing.

Danny didn't take himself too seriously. He was a joker at heart and I liked that about him. I wasted so much time trying to guess what other people were thinking about me. Danny just didn't give a shit.

"Who'd you think I was?" I asked.

"I don't know. I stepped on some guy's toes tonight," he said, walking over to me.

Danny looked trashed. He had a long, lean face and Kris's sloping cheekbones, but his eyes were bloodshot and the color had drained out of his lips. His hair was short and choppy and scattered.

"You should try Milk Duds," he said, grinning at the empty bag in my hands. "You'd get better accuracy."

"Thanks for the tip." I felt like such a jackass. Could he tell how desperate I was?

"No sweat." He sat down on the sidewalk and leaned up against the metal gate surrounding the front of his house. I noticed that his pants were ripped at the cuffs and he was missing a sock.

"You have a key?"

"I did when I left the house," he said. "Don't worry, this will wake her up." He stood up and walked into the street. "KRIS," he screamed. Looking up at her window, Danny shouted her name again just like Stanley Kowalski in New Orleans.

A window flew open on the second floor of another building and an overweight man in a white T-shirt stuck his head out. "Shut the fuck up!" he yelled and slammed his window shut.

"'Morning, Cowboy," Kris said, looking down at me.

She was leaning out her window in a terrycloth bathrobe and her hands were resting on the windowsill. She looked half asleep but her drowsy smile still jumpstarted my pulse. I didn't know why but Kris always seemed to fill this hole in my gut. I wasn't afraid of anything when I was with her except saying good night.

"I'm locked out," Danny hollered, trying to get her attention.

"What are you doing with Nick?" she said.

"We bumped into each other," he shouted.

"I'll be down in five." She ducked her head back inside.

I turned to Danny. "So, what've you been up to all night?" I asked, trying to hide my excitement.

"We were just chasing skirts." Danny unscrewed the cap on his High Life. "What about you?"

"Went to a movie," I mumbled. "What happened to your sock?"

"That's what I'd like to know," he said, taking a healthy gulp from his beer.

"You don't remember?"

"Hey, if I remember what I did, I feel gypped."

Kris's mother sent Danny off to rehab six months ago. The dean of his school caught him selling drugs and threatened to throw him out if he didn't go to a treatment center. Danny still denies being a drug dealer. According to him, he didn't make a cent—he wasn't selling, he was sharing.

Danny was so drunk and high on his flight to rehab that when the people from the treatment center picked him up at the airport, he had seven flight safety instruction cards, no wallet, and an empty bottle of Ativan. Danny doesn't remember the flight very well, but he claims he walked up and down the aisles buying the cards from other passengers. He says he just wanted to feel safe.

Now Danny pursed his lips tightly and inhaled deeply through his nose. "But see, this whole thing tonight wasn't my fault."

"Fine," I said, smiling. "You're completely innocent."

"Well, we're hanging out at this party with some good-looking girls, having a pretty big time. I mean, I couldn't believe how many there were, and there were only like five guys," Danny said. "I should've known something was wrong, but I just thought I was lucky."

"So I start talking to this girl, Jessica, you know, about nothing in particular. She went to one of those girls' schools named after some bird. Well, she was pretty drunk already, and I was fucking gone. So eventually, she says she's going to be sick and she asks me to come to the bathroom with her.

"She doesn't throw up, but I stayed with her to make sure she was okay. Then she tries to stand up and starts to fall over. I catch her on the way down, and we both hit the floor," Danny said, leaning over as if to imitate his fall. "And we go at it like nobody's business."

"This doesn't sound awful," I said.

"So she goes down on me and starts giving me the classic Easthampton blow job."

"I think that's called a hand job."

"Exactly. It's downright un-American." Danny sighed. "So everything's prim and proper until my friend comes in and starts screaming at me that this whole crew from Bruckner just showed up and the leader is looking for Jessica. Have you ever heard of the crew MKII?"

"Sure. Jessica must be Derrick Small's girl," I said, concerned.

Danny nodded. "Yeah, Derrick's his name."

"Derrick's out of his fucking mind. Memorial Day weekend, he stabbed some kid from Troy in the arm for buffing his tag." Most prep-school hoods just get high and crash parties, but kids like Derrick live to throw down and bleed you.

"Well, I didn't know square one. So I asked Jessica if he's her boyfriend, and she just starts laughing and reaching for her nose candy. Right there on the fucking floor. I bug out, throw on my shirt, and run down the back staircase with a hard-on. It's fucking difficult to run with a hard-on."

"No shit. How many hoods were there?"

"A dozen too many."

"Did they see you?" I asked. Danny didn't realize how crazy these kids were.

"I don't think so."

"So you made it out?"

"Yeah, but I just called one of the guys who went to the party with me. They messed him up pretty badly," Danny said, shaking his head. "Cut up his hands with a butterfly knife."

The toughest hoods in Manhattan's prep schools aren't like

other street thugs. They aren't poor and angry—they're just angry. They aren't outsiders; none of them have spent their lives trying to make it out of anywhere. They go to the best schools and spend their summers in the Hamptons.

Prep-school hoods try to dress just like hoods from Harlem and Brooklyn, except their clothing is always brand-new designer-label. Their chinos are usually a size too big, so that they hang loosely at the hips and bunch up around their Timberland boots, and bright Tag Heuers are on all their wrists. They normally wear a Tommy Hilfiger or Polo shirt with a nice-size label, and a North Face jacket, hood and all. Some of them even sport crest rings. They're kind of funny to watch, most of the time, until they decide to put somebody in the hospital.

"I hate those guys," I said. "They could never piece. All they ever want to do is fuck people up."

Danny laughed. "I forgot I was talking to the all-city graffiti prodigy."

"I retired a couple years ago," I muttered.

I used to write *DOA*. On the walls of the West Side Highway, in abandoned subway tunnels, and just about everywhere else I went. My two best friends and I were a three-man crew. Greg Carmichael tagged *LUST* and Charlie "Kodak" Kohl would usually work fill-ins or run surveillance. For a while, the three of us felt like kings instead of sophomores.

"You still have two pieces up though, right?"

"Just one on Twenty-second," I said, wondering if Danny knew why I'd given it all up. I didn't feel like talking about that night—I never do.

"You got crossed out?" Danny asked.

"Nah, they tore the building down. The piece was a fucking antique anyway."

"I can't imagine you as one of those hoods."

"I was never about jumping kids or dealing," I said, shrugging. "All I cared about was the art and street cred." These days, piecing seems like an afterthought for most prep-school hoods. They all tag mailboxes and benches, but they're in it for the attitudes and protection, the styles. I lived for the paint.

"Did you dress like them?"

"I guess. It's not that simple," I said, trying to push it out of my mind. I didn't want to think about anything but Kris.

Danny looked up at Kris's window. "Where the hell is she?" he cried. "I gotta piss like a racehorse."

Kris opened the door to her building and smiled sleepily at both of us. "You look like hell, Danny."

Danny looked down at his blue oxford and noticed a tear in the right sleeve. "I thought I looked preppie."

Kris sighed. "You're such a little rebel."

"Shantih shantih shantih," Danny said, walking into their townhouse.

Kris closed the door behind him and then walked down the steps. "What's going on?"

"Couldn't sleep," I said, wondering how ridiculous it sounded. Seeing me on her steps at four-thirty in the morning, she must've known something was haunting me. She just didn't realize who it was.

Kris sat down next to me. She twisted her hair into a clumsy ponytail and pushed her bangs away from her eyes. Our knees were barely touching.

Kris yawned into her palm. "Weren't you supposed to take that girl out tonight?"

"Waste of time." I leaned back against her steps. "I bailed after dinner."

Kris looked over at me, as if she was about to say something. I didn't move. Not an inch.

"That sucks," she said. "What'd you do all night then?"

"Hung out with Tim." Tim was my best friend at Daley, and it seemed like the easiest thing to say.

I always told Kris the truth about dates and hookups, just in PG-13. We'd spent whole afternoons dissecting some girl's flirty chatter or ambiguous e-mails. Most of the time, it was more fun to tell Kris about the date than it was to actually go on it. But sitting there next to her, breathing in her apple-scented shampoo, I just wanted Kris to think about us.

I turned toward her and studied her expression. I had no idea how to begin. "Sometimes I feel like I have no idea what I'm doing. You know?"

Kris grinned and looked at her watch. "I think you're waking me up at four-thirty-six in the morning."

I forced a smile. Those weren't the words I wanted to hear. She was supposed to say, *I know why you're here* or *I'm glad you're here.*

"I just needed to talk to somebody." I took a full breath and studied the cracks in the sidewalk. "What'd you do tonight?"

"Hung out with Tracy and her new boyfriend for a while. Tracy always makes herself out to be such a bimbo when she gets around a guy she likes. I mean, she's twice as bright as those mouth-breathers she dates, but she never shows it."

What was I waiting for? "It's understandable, though."

"That's crazy. What's she going to do, spend her whole life studying *Cosmo*'s 'Dos and Don'ts'?"

"You could talk to her."

"I have," Kris shook her head. "She just says it's different for me because I was with Luke for so long. I got so sick of them that I went home and read."

I pinched a cigarette and tucked it in the corner of my mouth. "Do you ever feel like that was mistake? I mean, to stay with Luke for so long."

She scrunched her pale forehead and tilted her jaw. "I don't think about it in terms of rights and wrongs. The way I see it, I was supposed to be with Luke for as long as I was. And now I guess I'm supposed to be alone for a while."

I stared down the street at the traffic signals, searching for some sort of response to the word "alone." I felt like lifting the collar of my sweater onto the bridge of my nose and hiding my face.

"Still on *The Sound and the Fury*?" I said, embarrassed by my own silence.

"Finished it yesterday. I just started *Two Years Before the Mast*."

I shrugged my shoulders. "Never heard of it."

"It was written in like 1840," Kris said. "By this rich kid who left Harvard to work on a ship."

"He was failing out?"

"No, he was losing his eyesight, so he had to drop out."

"Do you think I could try that?" I said, turning toward her and tapping my finger on the metal frame of my glasses.

Kris leaned toward me and squinted. She grinned and rubbed her finger softly against my cheek. "Your date couldn't have gone *that* badly."

Why hadn't I checked? Dropping my eyes to the pavement, I wiped the rest of the lipstick off my cheek and tried to smile.

Saturday

Nicholas." My mother's voice pressed against the door. "It's nearly one."

"It's Saturday," I said, pulling the covers over my head. "Let me sleep. Please."

———

"Nicholas."

I sat up, startled, and looked at my alarm clock. 1:10 P.M. "What?"

"Gloria needs to get in to clean your room."

"She cleaned it yesterday," I groaned. Why did we have to do this every fucking weekend?

I didn't have much in my room. A long black desk, a drafting board, a chest of drawers, a laptop, a television and DVD player, a bookshelf filled with nearly three hundred DVDs, and two old movie posters from *The Hustler*. None of it needed dusting.

"Nicholas, she needs to vacuum." The doorknob clicked, but it didn't open. I'd locked it when I came home last night.

"She vacuumed yesterday." Why couldn't she just leave me alone?

"What?"

"Ask her." I pulled the pillow out from underneath my head, rolled onto my side, and covered my ears. I felt like screaming at her, but that would only wake me up.

"Nicholas?" The doorknob clicked again. "Will you unlock the door?"

——

"Nick, it's Elliot." My stepfather. Prick. "It's half-past one, Nick. Your mother wants you out of bed."

She wasn't going to give up. She never did.

"Nick?"

I threw the covers off my bed and jumped up to unlock the door. Walking into the bathroom, I grabbed my toothbrush. My throat was killing me from all the cigarettes I'd smoked last night.

My mother married Elliot four years ago and we moved into his apartment on 76th and Park Avenue. When you live on Park, your sense of reality gets a little warped. Food and shelter are problems for the maid and the interior decorator. Everyone has a doorman; the very rich have two. People are just as miserable, though. They just have more expensive tissues to cry into.

I could hear my mother walk into my room. "She did vacuum yesterday. Huh."

"I told you," I said through a mouthful of toothpaste. This was worse than the hangover.

"Nick, your room smells like an ashtray."

I didn't say anything. My mother was always ragging on me for smoking. The quickest way to get through it was to not respond. I know what cigarettes do—I just don't give a shit.

"I'll have Gloria make you some eggs. . . ." Her voice faded.

"I'm not hungry," I said, walking back into the bedroom. I picked up my white T-shirt from last night and wiped my face dry. "I'm really not."

"Why won't you use a towel?" She sighed. My mother was standing in the middle of my room in the dark blue jumpsuit that she wore to the health club. Her second facelift had taken care of the wrinkles on her forehead, but she still carried around this worried expression, like something was about to start burning in another room.

"I can't stand them." A couple of weeks ago, Elliot had had all my towels monogrammed. I thought I was angry until I saw Elliot's face when I refused to thank him. It was great watching the veins in his neck swell.

"You're being ridiculous. I want you to eat something now, because I'm going to the office in a little bit and so is Elliot."

My mother worked part-time for the Asian art division at Sotheby's and seemed to be stuck in her own perpetual cocktail party. Her job was to know which families were buyers, which families were sellers, and which families would never do anything but drink and talk big.

"Scrambled," I said, diving back onto my bed. I loved my comforter. It could heat me up like a coal in five minutes flat.

"Don't fall back asleep," my mother said, walking out into the hallway.

—

My phone rang and I sat up in bed, hoping it was Kris. On the weekends, she usually called me around two, but I wasn't sure if she was annoyed about last night. I lifted the phone off the hook and placed it between the pillow and my ear.

"Hey, there," Kris said, through the static. This was my favorite way to begin the day. Some Saturdays I waited for her call to wake me like a bedside kiss.

"'Morning, Kris," I whispered.

"I'm walking across the park. You wanna meet at the spot in half an hour?"

"Kool and the Gang," I said, relieved. Most weekends, Kris and I went to this one giant evergreen in Central Park to hang out.

"Later." Kris was better than a hot cup of coffee.

I've only had one real girlfriend, Jamie Murphy. Sophomore year, our English teacher paired us up for an in-class presentation on *Henry V.* I don't know whether it was the third-floor cubicles or the St. Crispin's Day speech, but Jamie and I ended up dating for the next two months. We spent most of our time together working on our kissing—on her roof, in taxis, at school. I knew it wasn't love but she had these freckled, Irish cheeks and the cutest little smile I've ever seen. Then Jamie went on a July Teen Tour in France and met some guy who spoke a few more languages than I did. It chipped my pride but I guess we'd run out of places to neck.

As I reached to hang up the phone, I noticed the pulsing glow of my answering machine. *"One new message. First message left at 12:35 P.M.: Hey, it's Tim. If you don't make it to hoops, you should come to Sara's bash with Nancy and me. I promised her a party. Otherwise I wouldn't go near the place. And hey, I'm trying to remember the lyrics to that diarrhea song. You remember. First rhymes with* burst, third *is* turd, home *and* foam, *but what the hell is* second? *I leave you with this question, señor: what is* second?"

I grabbed a clean white T-shirt from my top drawer, put my jeans back on, and laced my Kenneth Coles. Checking myself in the mirror, I fixed my hair. With Kris I had to make sure that I looked good, but I couldn't try too hard or she might notice.

I walked down the hallway and headed toward the kitchen. Like every other top-shelf apartment on the Upper East Side, Elliot's place was decorated to entertain other people. Up until a year ago, I wasn't even allowed to hang out in the dining room unless there was company over. Elliot and my mother never said it outright, but if he caught me studying in there, he'd always ask, "Isn't there another room you could do that in?" It sucks not being able to relax in your own home.

Kris says she could never live on the Upper East Side after growing up on the Upper West Side, but there's no real difference. West Siders call their maids "housekeepers," and they drive Volvos instead of Mercedes. The gig's the same, though. Wealthy West Siders and East Siders may spend their summers on different beaches, but they'll both lecture the doorman if he doesn't open their cab door.

Elliot was sitting at the kitchen table in the red silk bathrobe that let everyone know he was relaxing. He had a bowl of cereal resting on top of his copy of *Barron's* and he didn't seem to notice that I'd walked in. Elliot worked downtown for Pierce & Pierce Investments. He spent so many hours in his office making money that he never had time to buy anything except squash rackets.

I got a fork out of the dishwasher and Gloria, Elliot's Costa Rican maid, handed me my plate. I nodded thanks and grabbed a carton of orange juice off the counter.

"Hey, he's up," Elliot said to nobody in particular.

My real father was an oil guy. At least that's what people said. He was a surveyor for companies looking for new places to drill. When people heard a rumor, they needed a guy to go check it out. Any suit could fly to Canada or Russia, but the oil execs wouldn't go to third-world countries or places that weren't even countries anymore. My father would.

"Knicks won pretty big," Elliot mumbled. "They're finally stepping up."

"Yup," I said, sitting down at the table.

"Some new guard."

"Yup."

I don't know if my dad ever realized it, but my mother would start crying as soon as he left on a trip. She would never let on while he was getting ready; sometimes she would even look excited. But as soon as the door closed behind him, she'd scoop me up, lie down on their bed, and just sob. I almost always ended up crying along with her. When you're a kid, there's nothing more terrifying than watching your mother weep.

If my dad came back in the middle of the night, he'd always sleep on the living-room floor. He said it was because he didn't want to wake my mother, but I think he had trouble sleeping in beds after a trip. I loved dragging the quilt off my bed and lying down next to him on our rug. I'd sniff at his palms and shirt to try and guess how long he'd gone without a shower. He'd always run his hands through my hair and tug softly at my ears. My dad loved my ears because the lobes were perfect semicircles like his.

"Martinez something," Elliot continued.

"Huh." I never knew what else to say.

My mother would always find my dad and me asleep on the floor. All morning I'd beg him to tell me what he'd found or who he'd met, and he'd spin these long tales about hiking across a deserted island, or camping in a rain forest, or trading his watch for a bowl of soup. Looking back, I wonder how many of them were actually true and how many were cooked up for my eight-year-old imagination. I guess it doesn't really matter. Sitting at our kitchen table, chomping on sugar cereal, he was my own personal Superman.

"How's your Spanish class at Daley?"

"It's okay. The teacher's not very good."

"Not very good?" Elliot said, looking down at his article.

Then there were the times when my dad didn't come back looking so well. Three days into Colombia, the wrong bug bit him, and he spent the next two shivering in a dugout canoe being paddled slowly upriver by a guy he'd just met. When we visited him in the hospital, his skin had turned a soft green. I remember sitting next to him, studying the scars on his hands, while my mother screamed down linoleum hallways at doctors. I thought I was going to throw up all over his bedspread.

"But as I recall, you liked last year's teacher," Elliot said. "Good marks at least."

"She doesn't teach seniors."

And then two weeks before my eleventh birthday, my mother told me that my dad wasn't coming back, that he was dead. I was halfway through an egg roll, staring at *The Simpsons,* when she started talking. I don't remember a single word she said. I couldn't hear her. Suddenly, I wanted to punch something. Hard. What had we done wrong? I didn't even realize that I'd started peeing until I smelled the sour heat of my damp sock.

I dropped my egg roll and ran into the bathroom. Turning the shower on, I climbed into the bathtub and lay down underneath the cool water. I tried to catch my breath as I waited for my mother's slow, predictable knock. How could she be sure? My pants started to stick to my thighs and butt, and I lay there wishing and crying.

I couldn't hear anything for weeks, or maybe I just couldn't listen. People would be talking at me, teachers, friends, bus drivers, and I wouldn't get it. The only place I could actually relax was in bed. If I left a couple sandwiches on my nightstand, I could sleep for ten or twelve hours at a time. My dad and I would talk sometimes in my sleep, but we always discussed the most random things, like the Beatles or potato chips or crosstown buses. I loved listening to his scratchy voice. I missed everything about him, always.

"Use a glass, Nick," my mother said, walking into the kitchen. "That's why we have them."

"Sorry," I muttered.

"You've got to get on a normal schedule," she continued. "You're really burning the candle—"

"I know," I interrupted.

After my dad died, everyone kept asking me to cry. My mother would always tell me that it was completely normal, and my teachers liked to remind me that I could excuse myself from class without permission. The school shrink explained that it was okay to "lose it" or "break down," but I still don't understand what he meant or how I would even know. Everywhere I went, people kept saying that I didn't have to put up a front.

I was terrified of tearing up around my teachers. The few times I actually did, they started nodding and sighing and saying they understood. Why can't people just listen without throwing in their two cents? I couldn't tell my teachers that my dad was the only person who understood how much I loved him. My dad knew how I would save all my embarrassing questions for our walks to the video store and how I used to cover for him when my mother got annoyed. He was the only person who ever really tried to understand me.

"I was thinking about your plans for next summer," Elliot said, looking over at me.

I wasn't. "Yeah."

And then the women started to show up. I don't know how many came, but they seemed to arrive in bunches. I met one. The doorbell had rung and I ran to answer it, ready to pay for a large pizza with sausage and green peppers. A tall woman with hazel eyes stared down at me and said my full name, balancing each syllable evenly on her tongue. I remember thinking that I'd won something. My mother rushed me into my bedroom, and I spent the next hour lying silently against the doorframe, listening to their conversation. The women usually brought something of my father's, a sweater or handkerchief, and there were always letters, lots of letters.

I just couldn't believe we weren't enough for him.

"Well," Elliot continued. "I was speaking with a partner of mine whose son spent the summer working on the floor."

"The floor?" I said innocently, shoveling the last of my eggs into my mouth.

"Of the stock exchange." Elliot sighed. "You know what I mean."

"Huh." I'd rather give myself paper cuts all day. When you have money and everything still sucks most of the time, you don't want to spend your life just making more.

"Nick, you need to work for your happiness," Elliot said, closing his newspaper.

A year after my dad died, my mother met Elliot at some hospital fundraiser. He'd spent most of his adult life in front of a computer screen and was looking to start a family; my mother was looking to save one. She told me their marriage was about me and my future, but she wanted the security, the stability. Elliot was a rock, and he wasn't going anywhere. It didn't matter that he was an asshole.

For the first two years of their marriage, Elliot and my mother fought practically every night. Sometimes they'd argue about his eighty-hour weeks; other times it was weekend plans, but it was always in their room, always late. That's how I got into the habit of falling asleep to movies. I'd buy a new one every day after school and leave it playing. It helped me relax. Eventually the fighting tapered off. No divorce, though, just resignation.

These days when I can't stand dealing with Elliot and his attitude, I'll call Kris and tell her that there's this movie I have to show her. She usually lets me come over, even if she has a lot of homework to do. A couple weeks ago, I watched all three hours of *The Good, the Bad, and the Ugly* while she wrote a term paper on Morocco. I think she knows I'm there because I don't know where else to go.

———

The breeze jogged by me down Fifth Avenue and swept the leaves into whirlpools of candy-bar wrappers and plastic bags. October was settling into Central Park, but the afternoon still had the sweet scent of August. I was just glad to be out of the apartment and away from the two of them.

I stopped at the hot-dog stand right outside the 72nd Street park entrance and bought a Coke. I had a few minutes to kill before I was supposed to meet Kris. Sitting down on a chipped bench, I took a long, hard drag on the day's first cigarette. It was always the best. I should have looked around before I sat down, but I didn't, and so I never saw Greg Carmichael until he was ten feet from my bench wearing his typical, obnoxious grin.

"Thet," he shouted. We hadn't bumped into each other in months, but Greg never passed up a chance to try and show me up.

I nodded "hello." Greg and Kodak had given me the nickname Thet, because *DOA* was just a little too suspicious and my *O* came out as a perfect theta. They told our teachers it was because I was the top Greek student, but all the other guys in our grade knew the truth. And pretty soon Thet had more street cred than any prep-school hood in Collier history.

"Yo, what you doing here?" Greg cried. He walked over to me, throwing his shoulder into each stride like a hood thinks he has to. Greg had a thick jaw and restless, green eyes, and he was wearing a baggy Polo sweatshirt.

"Meeting somebody," I said. "What about you?"

I'd started hanging out with Greg in seventh grade at the Collier School for Boys. After my mother and I moved into Elliot's place, I always avoided going back to Elliot's apartment. Most days after school, Greg, Kodak, and I would smoke a joint in Central Park and go to Greg's building to watch television. He had five twenty-seven-inch Sony TVs hanging in his room and a DIRECTV dish strapped to the roof of his building. Greg was obsessed with sports and gambling on sports, and he said the only way he could relax was to have all the games playing at once. Greg always used to say that his goal in life was to set the odds in Vegas, but lying on his couch half-stoned, all I wanted to do was forget about tomorrow. I'd get sick of *SportsCenter* sometimes, but it was always better than listening to Elliot.

"Some guys and I just did some Benzos, and we figured we'd come here and chill. You know, until Sara's party starts and shit."

I nodded again. Why couldn't he just keep walking?

"So who you meeting?" Greg asked.

"Kris Conway."

"Mad cute, goes to school downtown?"

"Yeah," I said, surprised he recognized her name. I guess she was *that* beautiful.

"She's chill. A little JAPy for my styles, but I bet she likes your loafers," he said, smirking at my shoes.

I brushed it off. "I'm not sure she's noticed."

"She your womans?"

"Just friends," I said, hating the sound of it.

"Too bad, boy. You gotta be able to convert that shit. Break it in like a glove."

I didn't respond. Watching Greg flex his attitude, it was hard for me to believe we'd ever been friends.

At the end of eighth grade, Greg, Kodak, and I had started tagging, just doing fat-cap throwies and trying not to get busted. Most of the Collier boys tagged a handful of bus stops and quit, but I loved the rush. Working the sides of buildings, ducking the cops, racing frantically to beat the sunrise—the three of us had found a cause. It was more fun than art class at Collier, and all the training finally paid off. I caught a rep beyond the Upper East Side. Suddenly, girls I'd never met before knew my tag, and kids were always going out of their way to invite Thet to their parties. I felt like a fucking movie star.

I pushed open the fireproof back door of my building and stepped outside into five in the morning. Kodak tossed our red laundry bag into my chest and I caught it with my free hand.

"Fuck, it's early," I said, kicking off my penny loafers. My whole body was stiff. I dropped the bag to the pavement and started unbuttoning my oxford.

"I got you a Pop-Tart," Kodak said, chewing. A canvas mini-duffel rested on both his shoulders like a backpack and he was balancing two cartons of orange juice in his right hand.

"I'm good." I pulled my hoodie out of the laundry and stuffed my tie and blazer into the sack. I reached for the second Tropicana. "Thanks."

"You're not supposed to go to work on an empty stomach," Kodak said, frowning playfully. He had nervous, brown eyes and the kind of frame that didn't win you any favors.

"Says who?"

"The FDA, is who."

"That includes graf artists?" You had to love a kid who wouldn't go bombing on an empty stomach.

Kodak dug his fist into the laundry bag and slid out my stained jeans. They were glazed with paint and dirt, but they were still the prettiest piece of clothing I owned. I stepped out of my charcoal slacks and felt the side-street breeze hit my boxers.

"So Lusty rolled it?" I asked. Last night, Greg was supposed to take a paint roller and a can of Ivory White to a parking lot wall on 95th and Third. We had our routine down—get dressed for school, change, work, and be back in shirt and tie by first bell. It was exhausting, but I lived for it.

Kodak nodded and ran his hand over his crewcut. "That's what he says."

"Well, I racked six cans off Woolworth's," I said, pulling up my jeans.

We were Krylon boys—Sparkly Gray and Midnight Blue were my primaries. I'd write the half-circle of the D, the O, and the two legs of the A. Then I'd run the intersecting line of the A, through the middle of the O, and spread it out to form the D with an arrowhead.

"I've still got two blacks and half a red." Kodak stared up at the high-rises. "How many pieces you gonna put up?"

"Just one," I said, adjusting my belt. *I could work on a single piece for an hour, tweaking the fades and shadows until I ran out of paint.*

Kodak grinned. "Dream big."

I smiled and stretched my neck. On a morning like this, there was nothing better than burning through six cans, getting narced on the fumes, and smoking a cigarette.

———

"Hey, you see my new piece?" Greg said excitedly.

I shook my head. "Must've missed it."

Greg smiled. He knew I didn't give a shit. "It's this dope green and silver down on Forty-third. Your old school styles, but without getting sloppy."

"I'm glad to hear you're leaving the stencils at home."

"Oh, well excuse your punk ass." Greg leaned toward me. He wasn't going to throw down but I could feel my chest tighten. "You must think this is old-timers day or some shit."

I shrugged it off. "Something like that," I muttered. I hadn't touched a can of paint in nearly two years, but Greg could never touch my wildstyles and he knew it.

"Like Kodie didn't run your fill-ins, too," Greg declared, trying to stare me down.

"Yup," I said, the inflection in my voice suddenly dropping. I looked over at the park entrance. I had to get the hell away from him.

"You know Kodak was in town last weekend," Greg said.

"What? For real?"

"Yeah." Greg nodded. "Some of my boyz saw him on West End."

"I—"

"Expected a phone call or some shit, right?" he sneered.

I didn't know what to say. For years, I'd been replaying that night, frame by frame, trying to splice it back together.

"So I guess I'll see you later in time," Greg said. He'd won, and he knew it.

Greg walked off toward the Reservoir and I took a full breath. My cigarette had curved into a long, flimsy ash—I'd forgotten about it. Dropping the butt, I pounded it into the concrete. I didn't need to start thinking about Kodak and the whole damn mess.

The Collier boys had given Kodak his nickname in fifth grade when he was caught documenting the early stages of his pubescence on film. Apparently, the guy at the One-Hour Photo called the cops because he thought it was a child pornography ring. Eventually, Kodak's thirteen-month study was subpoenaed.

Kodak and I'd become best friends at the beginning of sixth grade. Two weeks into first semester, his au pair rolled their Range Rover across three lanes of the L.I.E. and into oncoming traffic—his sister died instantly. After the accident, Kodak and I started hanging out and talking about family and life and everything else that was on our minds. He was a virtuoso cellist, and we used to cut gym and work on his concertos. I loved sitting in that empty auditorium, watching his hands wiggle and twist through a piece. He'd always ask my opinion. Sometimes I think Kodak pretended like I knew what I was talking about just because we both needed the company. Besides, I was the only one in the grade who didn't shit on him for being good at something.

When I first started smoking up with Greg, he never wanted me to bring Kodak along. I couldn't explain why I trusted Kodak so much, so one night during eighth grade Greg and I split a bottle of Chivas and I forced him to watch *The Godfather*. When we were done, and flipping through the late games, I told him to think of Kodak as a consigliere, but with asthma. After that, the three of us were inseparable.

———

"So I made a list of things I could talk about with that girl, Patty," Kodak said, swinging the laundry bag over his shoulder.

"You're stressing, Kodie." I lifted my backpack and felt the weight of seventy-two ounces of Krylon. There was barely enough room for my textbooks.

We started walking toward Lexington and I checked my watch. 5:15 A.M. The streetlights would be on for another forty-five minutes. Then the garbage men would sail down the avenue. After them, you'd see stockbrokers and busboys.

"So what's on the list?" I said, sipping my orange juice.

"It's tentative," Kodak began. "But I was thinking about starting with cats."

"Cats?"

"Like the animal."

"You don't have any pets," I said.

"But I like them a lot," Kodak said, shrugging. "Besides, girls are supposed to love that sort of stuff."

"Okay."

"And, I mean, I really do like cats, Thet."

"Why don't you ask Dr. Rudas what to say?"

Kodak and I had mandatory weekly visits with the school shrink, Dr. Michael A. Rudas, and we both had to deal with the same bullshit metaphors and role plays. The only thing I learned from that doctor was that I wasn't a "car with a flat tire," or "a painter without brushes," or "a length of twisted rope."

"I did already," Kodak said, ignoring my sarcasm. "I think I ran out of things to lie about."

"So what'd he say?" I laughed.

"Not much. He kept asking me why Patty made me so nervous. Then that started to make me nervous."

"That's why I'm sticking with the program."

Kodak and I had a bunch of different strategies to protect ourselves against the shrink. Dr. Rudas had a habit of scribbling away on his notepad during our sessions, so Kodak and I started rehearsing our comments and responses. We knew the less he had to work with, the safer we were, but we didn't hide shit from each other. I was the only person who knew that Kodak was also supposed to be in that car, that he would've sat shotgun, that he would've died instead, *and Kodak was the only one I told about my conversations with my dad.*

If Kodak and I ran out of prepared material, we'd start bullshitting about the Yankees or homework assignments. I could always fall back on old movies or random directors, and Kodak mastered the art of just sitting there and acting pale. Dr. Rudas would've given his pinky finger to know half the shit Kodak and I talked about, but we were unbreakable.

▬

I saw Kris as soon as I hit the lawn near the Alice in Wonderland statue. The park was littered with joggers and drifting toddlers, but Kris sat completely still at the base of our giant evergreen, like she was pulling everybody else's strings. Halfway across the lawn, Kris spotted me and waved. I felt Kris's eyes taking my stride in and I started to watch myself from her point of view. My footsteps: soft heel then toe. My hands: stuffed in my pockets, thumbs dangling just outside. My shoulders: tense. Sometimes I felt like her eyes were the only lenses that mattered.

"Anybody else wake you up last night?" I said, looking for a smile.

"Yeah." Kris laughed and lay down like she was sunbathing in the shade. "Con Ed at, like, six in the morning." She skipped a stone across the lawn.

I leaned up against the gnarled trunk of the evergreen. The base of the tree was scattered with our squashed cigarette butts and an occasional bottle cap. It's important to have your own spot.

I'd eventually told Kris about Victoria and the kiss, but she still had no idea what was really going on inside me. "That's never happened to me before," I said, scratching at the bark. "You think I'm going crazy?"

Kris grinned. "I think *you're* waking up, Cowboy. You shouldn't have gone back to her apartment in the first place."

I kept my gaze firmly planted on the ground. "Girls are just much cooler in my head," I said, annoyed. "Before we go out."

"How do you mean?"

"I don't know." I sat down and tugged at a clump of grass. "Like if I don't know what type of music she's into, I imagine she likes my favorite Coltrane album. No, even better, that's all she listens to. And then before I know it, I've built her up into Grace Kelly."

"Instead of a senior who decapitates hamsters."

"You get the point."

"Nick, I think you watch too many movies."

"That's funny." I sighed and dropped the blades of grass into the breeze. "I don't think I watch enough."

Kris smiled and wrapped the stem of a leaf around her finger. "It's not reality, Cowboy."

"Yes, it is," I declared. "It's just a nicer reality."

I scanned the lawn, searching the tree line for Greg's tailored step. I could still feel that anxious buzz in my palms and fingertips. Why the fuck couldn't I shut Greg out? I stretched my arms in the air and filled my lungs.

Kris leaned toward me. "Are you okay, Nick?"

"Yeah," I said, surprised. "Why?"

"You just seem kind of on edge or something."

"I'm cool," I said, trying to push Greg and Kodak out of my mind. Kris knew some of the history but I couldn't handle rehashing all that baggage. Besides, hanging out with Kris was the best antidote I had. "Maybe a little hungover."

Kris looked right through me. "Where do you go when you look like that?"

"Like what?"

"You know what I mean. You get this really serious look on your face . . . I guess you've always had it. Let's call it Nickville," Kris said, grinning.

"Why?"

"Because you're stuck in your head, Cowboy."

"You're probably right."

"What are you thinking about? I mean, what's going on in Nickville?"

"I don't know. Sometimes I just have no idea how I'm going to make sense of everything. It's like I start thinking and I feel totally overwhelmed and . . . it's completely . . . I don't know," I said, trying to decide if she bought my explanation.

"Nickville sucks."

"Sometimes. It rains a lot there." I surveyed the park again.

A terrier prowling around a small patch of grass took off in a flat sprint after a squirrel, around two oaks and under a bench. Finally, the squirrel made a sharp turn that the terrier couldn't.

I wanted the afternoon to be about Kris and me, but I couldn't stop wondering why Kodak hadn't called me last weekend. "I ran into Greg," I said, looking over at Kris. "Right before we met."

She nodded understandingly. "What'd he say?"

"Just the usual bullshit," I lied.

——

Greg and I slapped hands.

"Morning, boyz," Greg said, grabbing Kodak's hoodie and rubbing a nuggie into his scalp. Kodak elbowed him and Greg let him shake the hold.

I pulled my black book out of my backpack and flipped through the pages. I'd spent three hours last night sketching out my next piece, and I was dying to show Greg. The lettering was getting more jagged, more jigsawed, but I could never predict the color blends. I wanted the blues and reds to stream together, throughout the characters, but I wasn't going to force it. Besides, piecing was all about that spontaneous instant, when I saw something new and didn't hesitate.

I handed Greg the sketch and walked up to the white wall. Quik Park had leveled an old tenement in the middle of 95th Street and paved a concrete quadrangle. A pair of Chinese restaurants hugged the lot. Near the sidewalk, a convention of pigeons was working their way through last night's garbage. They were willing to share Third Avenue with us.

"This is dope," I whispered. The spot was perfect. From the street, everyone would see my wildstyles, but the angle of the buildings would keep us in the shadows for at least another hour. I needed four cans, five at the most. And suddenly it didn't matter anymore that it was five-thirty in the morning, that I had a Trig quiz first period— the piece was the only thing.

"Your shit's crazy angular," Greg said, handing me back the black book. "But it's mad chill."

"Thanks." I picked up my backpack and searched for my favorite *fat cap nozzle. I'd stolen it off a bottle of WD-40 or Lysol, and doctored it with a razor until I got the right effects. It was perfect for outlines.*

Flipping a can of Krylon Black into my right hand, I tossed it, end-over-end, like a martini shaker. I popped the top with my thumb and then swung my arm through the shadow of the first letter.

"Rolling," I said, turning back to Kodak and Greg. I felt like such a hero.

The paint hissed out of the can and smacked the wall. Every writer learns to love the sound of a full can. Some nights, after a movie has finished and the credits have rolled, the static on the television will nudge me awake, and I'll think for a second that I just cracked open a new canister.

Greg moved into the spot on my left. Dropping his backpack at the foot of the wall, he ran his palm across the damp brick.

———

Kris and I walked into the Slate just as dollar-drafts Happy Hour was ending. After the park, we'd killed a few hours in the Barnes & Noble on Broadway, just reading magazines and flipping through books. I'd found out about a ten o'clock revival showing of *The Sheltering Sky* at the Forum, and we figured we'd have a couple of well drinks at our favorite pub and then walk over.

The Slate was an NYU bar on 13th. It had a small stage in the back and a dozen wooden tables spread out across the floor. Most of the clientele were either underage or collecting Social Security. Even though the band was getting worse, the bar was filling up quickly. The singer had been trying to scat for the last few minutes, but she never really found her groove and ended up sounding more like Charlie Brown's teacher.

We found a small table in the back and flagged a waitress. I could tell that the two guys in front of us were talking about Kris. The first guy gave a quick nod to tip off his friend and the second guy turned nonchalantly around on his chair, like he was checking the clock on the wall. When the first guy shifted his glance over to me for a second, I smiled right back at him.

"I got a letter from Luke," Kris said. "He says hi."

Luke could kiss my ass. Why did he have to keep writing her? "Tell him I say hey."

"He was passing through Vermont. He had two gigs in Burlington," Kris said, sipping her beer. "He was talking about getting back on the water over the summer. I think he found a pretty nice boat to work on. They're going to Santa Cruz."

"Great." I just wanted him to get the hell out of my way.

Kris sat up and slid a crumpled letter from the back pocket of her jeans. As soon as I saw it, I felt like grabbing my pack of matches and torching it. She flipped through a couple of pages and then offered me the final sheet. I leaned forward slowly and lifted the flimsy paper from her palm.

"Tell me what you think he means," Kris said. "He can be so cryptic."

The page had a dozen creases across its body, like she'd been carrying it around with her since she opened it. At that moment, I would've paid somebody twenty bucks to trip the Slate's fire alarm.

I miss your shade, K. This country will wear you down
if you don't watch out. New Orleans, Memphis, St. Louis.
I keep trying to let my guard down (like you always tell

me to), but I'm not strong enough to handle the emptiness.
The highways are starting to play tricks on me, telling me
they're stronger than my music. But what's one more
burden on these shoulders? I'm doing the best I can, I
promise. . . . I can only sleep knowing that you believe me.
                                                    Love, Luke

"What's it mean, Cowboy?"

"Say no to drugs," I said, smiling.

"Very funny." Kris yanked the sheet out of my hand and tucked it back into her pocket. "He sounds really depressed."

I nodded. "Maybe he'll sort it out in his next letter," I said, trying not to sound bitter.

"Actually, he's supposed to be driving into the city tonight."

Fuck me. "Really. Why?"

"He wants to record some of his new songs. I think he's got some people pretty interested," Kris continued. "He sent me a couple pages of lyrics and there's a lot of great stuff about being on the road."

I sipped my Jameson and surveyed the crowd at the bar. "Good for him."

For the first eleven years of my life, I'd only seen my dad drink two types of booze, champagne and Jameson. Champagne was all he would touch on New Year's Eve, and Jameson owned the other three hundred and sixty-four days. My mother would usually cut him off after three drinks, but he'd sneak a few once she went to sleep. If I caught my dad by the liquor cabinet, he'd always fix me a splash. Jameson used to burn my throat and sinuses, but I loved sitting there next to him on the couch, clutching our little secret.

Kris waved her empty Amstel in the air until our waitress saw. "Do you want another whiskey?"

"I'm fine." I didn't want to drink too much early, or I'd end up praying to a porcelain god for a quick death.

"Kris," I began, just wanting to change the subject, "where do you see yourself in ten years?"

"I don't know. Can I have more than one choice or does that ruin it?"

"Two's the limit."

"Okay, I guess my first fantasy is to be a writer," Kris said. "But I could also see myself as a journalist who writes fiction on the side. You know, just so I have some money coming in if things didn't work out with my novels. But sometimes I worry that being a writer is too antisocial. I have this image of myself sitting in front of some old typewriter getting crazier and crazier. So even if I wrote a really good novel, I'd be so wacko that I wouldn't even be able to step outside my house. You know, like Salinger."

"And life number two?" I asked.

"I think I'd like to be a sailor, like in the America's Cup or the Whitbread."

"Do they let women?"

"Yes, buddy," Kris said, glaring at me. "Hell, I'd be just as happy racing Lasers or Hobies."

Kris's father had taught her how to sail as soon as she learned to swim. Their family used to own a house near Mystic, Connecticut, and they spent their summers there until her parents split up. Her father would take her out on all these different sailboats, and she kept logs and records of their trips. Kris says it's how she started writing in journals.

"So are you married during this writing or sailing career?"

"I don't think so," Kris said.

"Oh, come on," I said, biting down on an ice cube. "Don't you want some happily-ever-after guy?"

"I don't think I want to get married until I'm much older. I might live with some guy, but marriage . . . no, that's a ways off."

"Could you see yourself ending up with a guy like Luke?"

"I don't know. Definitely not Luke the way he is now." Kris sighed. "But who really knows anyway, right?"

"Right," I said, squeezing my glass.

"What about you, Cowboy? Where do you want to end up?"

I'd been thinking about it all day, and I'd decided that there would be approximately two seconds between when I told Kris that I was in love with her and she responded. It's amazing how I can let millions of seconds fade away but two seconds can be everything, two seconds can decide everything.

———

Sitting on the next stool, I placed Kris's lighter on her napkin. "Hi, I'm Nick."

"Kris," she said so softly that her name trickled into my ears. She slipped the lighter into her jacket.

"What are you writing?" I asked.

"It doesn't really matter."

"Are you writing a story or is it like a diary?"

"It's both." She gave me a look that said "Why are you still here?" but I didn't falter.

"Truth is stranger than fiction, you know," I said, trying hope-

lessly to liven up our conversation. If this didn't work, I was out of there. "It has to be. Fiction must be plausible."

Kris's head was bent over her book, and her hair was hiding most of her face, but I'll bet a lap around Central Park in the middle of the night that she smiled.

"You make that up yourself?"

"No, it's Mark Twain," I said, remembering when my dad first used that line on me.

"It's pretty funny." She hit the bottom of her soft pack and the tip of a cigarette popped out.

I reached quickly for the matches I had in my pocket and lit one using only my left hand. It was a trick I'd learned from Kodak, and I was so proud to show it to her.

"I thought you didn't have a light." Kris closed her diary, and my ego popped like a circus balloon. I wanted to say something cool to try and make up for it, but I couldn't think clearly. I felt like that poor kid who runs into the wrong end-zone with the football and celebrates.

"What did you say your name was?" Kris asked.

"Nick." I lowered my head. I don't know why, but her blue eyes scared the hell out of me. I was sure that if I looked into them, I wouldn't be able to find my way home.

"Remember yesterday when you sat in the corner booth?" I nodded and felt my cheeks heat up. "You sat there for nearly an hour. It was so ridiculous, it was kind of nice. And then when you came back tonight . . . I don't know."

"You saw me watching you?"

"There are mirrors all over this diner," she said, grinning.

"What should I have said?"

"I don't know. What kinds of lines do guys say these days?"

"I wish I knew," I muttered.

"How about 'Hi, my name's Nick. I was hoping to buy you a cup of coffee, and I have my own matches.'"

"Kris," I began, and I suddenly realized how nice it was to simply say her name.

—————

"Nick?"

"I don't know," I finally said to Kris and myself. "I can't even figure out what I want to do tomorrow."

"What about tonight?" Kris laughed.

"Seventy-millimeter screening of Storaro's best film." I couldn't handle listening to her talk about Luke. What was it going to take for me to stop being such a pussy? "You're going to love the print."

"Was he the director?"

"Cinematographer," I said, closing one eye.

Tim walked into the Slate with his hand comfortably wrapped around his girlfriend's waist. He nodded hello and pushed his way toward us. Normally, I wouldn't want to share Kris with anybody, but I'd talked myself into a corner.

Tim was a heavyset kid with a gentle smile and a soft, Georgia drawl. We were placed in the same sophomore advisory at Daley and we've hung out together ever since. After Greg and Kodak, I just wanted to keep things low-key. Tim didn't hang out with hoods—he wanted to be a comedian. And I could always count on Tim to split a six-pack and a pizza.

"What's going on, guys?" I said, pulling over two seats. Tim and Nancy had been going out for the last three months. I'd only hung out with her a couple times, but I could tell she was a sweet girl. She lived out on Long Island, and Tim was always talking about how she spent all her time working with blind children, or children of the blind, or something like that.

"Not much." Tim rested his hand on my shoulder. "Kris, this is Nancy. Nancy, Kris," he said, motioning with his fingertip. "How long have you guys been here?"

"About half an hour. Sorry about hoops this morning," I said, grinning. "Slept in."

The trumpet player stood up from his seat and started ruining an old Miles Davis tune. Nobody was listening anyway.

———

We paid and the four of us stepped onto 13th Street. There's this very distinct smell Manhattan gives off at night. People joke that it's a potpourri of trash, car exhaust, and urine, but to me it just smells like home. When I step onto the sidewalk and take a deep breath, I feel my heart jump. New York City is addictive.

"So what are you guys thinking about?" Tim walked into the street and raised his arm for a taxi. "Sara's party won't be that bad." Sara went to school in midtown with one of my old classmates from Collier.

"I think we're going to pass," I said, turning to Kris. "Sara's is going to be hood central."

"Thanks for the invite," Kris said to Tim.

"Yeah," I continued. "We're going to go check out this movie at the Forum—"

Kris turned to me. "Actually, I might just go home."

There were times when I couldn't tell if Kris was bored with me or the high school scene or life in general. Some nights we'd be getting along famously, and she'd bail to go read a book or write in her journal. I couldn't complain about it without making a complete ass of myself. If it were up to me, she'd never leave my side.

"Then let's just go hear some *real* music," I said. "Besides, I wouldn't mind another drink." I couldn't go home right now.

Tim flagged a cab and opened the door for Nancy. "Well, we're heading uptown. You guys want a lift?"

Kris checked her watch. "I kind of made plans to meet up with Luke later."

My chest hurt—my lips went numb. I felt like I was hanging upside down by my shoes and all the blood was running into my head.

"So you guys want to split this cab?" Tim shouted, from inside the taxi.

I didn't know what to say or think or anything. Kris could just unplug me without even realizing it.

"Why didn't you tell me earlier?" I said to Kris.

"I think it was the *'Say no to drugs'* comment." She grinned. "Why don't you go uptown with them? I just haven't seen him in a long time."

I felt like such a jackass. Not just because Kris was ditching me for Luke, but because it was happening in front of Tim and his girlfriend. Even the cabbie was watching.

"All right," I said, trying to regain my composure. "I'll give you a call tomorrow." I followed Tim into the taxi and gave Kris a good-bye nod. "Later."

"Later, guys," Kris said as she closed our cab door.

In less than a minute, I was a block away from Kris, sitting snugly next to Nancy. What the fuck was wrong with me? Why couldn't I stand up for myself?

"So you want to check out this party?" Tim asked.

And say something like "Stop."

"Nick, you want to come with us?"

Or just tell Kris the truth.

"With us, do you wanna come?" Tim cried, jokingly.

"Sorry," I said, shrugging it off. "Just drop me off at the diner on Eighty-second."

"You sure?"

"Yeah, I think I'm gonna crash early tonight." I didn't know what to do with myself, but I couldn't go with Tim and Nancy. I needed some time to sort everything out. All day I'd been thinking about telling Kris how I really felt, but I wasn't even sure that it mattered anymore.

Tim patted the back of my neck. "Man, you can fog over."

"I know. It's called Nickville."

"What?"

"Nothing." I laid my forehead against the cab window and closed my eyes. I was such a loser.

The driver sped across town, listening to the news in French and drumming a beat on the steering wheel.

"Kris went to see that guy she used to date?" Tim asked.

"Yeah."

"I'm sorry, kid." Tim rolled down his window. The cool

breeze wrapped around the back windshield and I suddenly felt all the sweat on my palms and neck.

"So am I."

———

The cab pulled up to the corner of 82nd Street, and Nancy gave me a long hug good night. I could see that she felt sorry for me. I guess that made two of us.

"I'll catch you guys later," I said, stepping out of the taxi.

The cab sped off. I reached quickly for a cigarette.

"Nick!"

I turned around and saw Danny leaning up against the phone booth just outside the Three Brothers diner. He was holding a large pizza box with one hand and trying to make a phone call. I didn't feel like talking to anybody, especially Kris's brother, but I couldn't ignore him now.

"What's up?" Danny said, tucking the pizza carton underneath his arm. I noticed a dark purple line running along his cheekbone. "How you doing?"

"You get popped?"

Danny nodded and showed me the Ray's Original pizza box. "You want pepperoni or broccoli? I ate all the anchovies."

"You okay?" I asked, waving off the pizza.

"That's a good question." Danny rocked back and forth on his toes. I'd never seen him this edgy before.

"What the hell happened?"

"MKII," Danny said exasperatedly. "They're really bitter fucking guys."

"I thought they didn't see you."

"I thought so, too." He reached down and pulled off his shoe. Then he slid his sock off and tried to hand it to me. I didn't want to touch it but he insisted. "Look at the bottom, Nick."

I turned the damp sock over. Danny's full name was written in green marker across the side.

"Mom," he groaned and gave this helpless smile. "She's so practical. She had the housekeeper label all my clothes when I went away to rehab."

My breathing quickened—he was fucked. "You left your sock behind?"

"I raced to get the hell out of there as soon as MKII showed up. Isn't that fucking ridiculous?"

"How'd you find out?"

"This girl from my history class called all worried about me. She'd heard MKII was putting together a manhunt. That they'd found my sock in the bathroom." Danny took a pepperoni slice out of the box and then dropped the carton to the ground. "There were three MKIIs sitting across the street from our house all afternoon. They started throwing bottles at the front door. Fucking derelicts."

Danny stared down at the glossy slice. "I can't eat this right now. You sure you don't want it?"

I shook my head. "MKII doesn't kid around." I didn't want to freak Danny out, but MKII made its name fucking kids up.

"No shit," Danny said, angrily kicking open the pizza box and tossing the slice back in.

"So what'd you do?"

"I snuck out the back and went over to my friend's house. You know, the one who got his hand cut up."

"And?"

"And there were two guys waiting outside his apartment building. I should've noticed their clothing, but I didn't think MKII was so fucking methodical. Well, one of them swings at me, these three old ladies start screaming 'POLICE, POLICE,' and I jetted."

"This definitely sets your personal record," I said.

"There's nothing wrong with having a couple nights that'll live in infamy." Danny slid his sock back on and laced his shoe. "I just don't want to get my face kicked in."

"Well, when they catch you, you'll be lucky if you don't end up in traction," I said disgustedly. When I'd stepped out of the cab, I'd been so pissed off at Kris and myself and Luke—suddenly I was furious at MKII. How dare they go after Danny?

"I know." Danny rubbed his finger against his cheekbone and squirmed. "Is Kris coming? I left her a message, but I figured she'd show up at the diner."

"She's with Luke," I said, looking down at the sidewalk. I hated saying his name.

"The granola-eating freak?"

"Yup."

"I think I have his number." Danny pulled out his wallet and slid a small, black address book out of a pocket. "I've got his father's loft."

"Let's try it," I said, placing a quarter in my palm and offering it to Danny. We slapped hands and the crisp sound shuttled down the block.

He dialed the number.

"Yeah . . . Hello . . . Yeah, can you hear me? Is Luke there? Well, when do you—No, see, I need to speak with him." Danny covered the receiver. "Fucking hippies," he groaned.

"No, tell him to stay home when he gets there . . . that Danny needs to talk to Kris. Can you do that, pal? It's an emergency. Okay, I can wait." Danny let the phone hang by the metal cord and rolled his eyes. "Burners, man. They're wastes of space."

"Bouncing wastes of space," I added.

Danny reached for the phone and pressed the receiver to his ear. "Okay, pal, just tell Luke and Kris to stay put. We'll call back when Jerry Garcia comes back to fucking life," he shouted, slamming the phone down. He was losing it, but I guess I couldn't blame him.

"You shouldn't have made that Jerry comment," I said, grinning.

"He was already hanging up the phone," Danny muttered. "So what's next?"

I shrugged. "I don't know. I'm pretty fried."

"There's got to be some way to outsmart these guys."

"These aren't the kind of guys you can just shake. I mean, they live for this shit."

"Well, I wouldn't fare well as an expatriate," Danny said. "Kris is going to kill me."

He was right. Danny was the only person Kris felt responsible for.

I had one idea, but it didn't make any sense. On the other hand, for the last twenty-four hours nothing had really made sense.

"There's one person I could call," I said. How could I be thinking about asking Greg for help? Just bumping into him had screwed up my whole afternoon. Fuck it. I couldn't feel any smaller than I already did. "Let me talk to an old friend of mine."

"Who's that?"

"You know a kid named Greg Carmichael?"

"Never heard of him."

After everything had fallen apart sophomore year, Greg and I were both suspended from Collier. My mother immediately transferred me to Daley, and Greg started a week later at Melville. I knew my writing days were over, but Greg never looked back. I don't even think he knew how to stop. He used his street cred to join a large Riverdale crew called the Dignitaries, or the Diggs for short. Everybody called them the Dicks behind their backs.

Greg had done everything he could to recruit me into the Diggs. He'd dragged me out with them once, and a bunch of the senior hoods had taken turns selling me on the girls and parties, the protection and brotherhood. I felt like I owed it to Greg, but I wasn't buying. It drove him crazy. For months, he'd call me up in the middle of the night, deliriously high, and start yelling at me for abandoning him, for being a pussy. Eventually, he gave up. I just didn't see the point of it all anymore.

"He's an old friend of mine, or whatever, and he knows about this sort of stuff." Who was I doing this for? Was it for Danny or Kris or me?

Danny rested his hands behind his head and took a long breath. "If it'll help."

"It might," I said. "He'll be at this girl's house party on Ninety-eighth."

"Well," Danny said, pointing uptown. "My calendar just opened up."

"Mine, too."

Danny and I walked up Lexington. The streets were filled with yuppies drinking and flirting their way down the avenue, and for the first time since I've known him, Danny had nothing to say. I could see how scared he was, and part of me just wanted to give him a hug.

"What'd you do all day?" I asked. "I mean, you couldn't go home."

"I snuck into this modern architecture lecture at the New School. Did you know Mies van der Rohe added the 'van der Rohe'?"

I shook my head. "They just let you sit in?"

"Yeah, I do it all the time. If you sit in the cheap seats nobody ever seems to care."

"You're crazy, Danny."

"Why?" he said. "I think it's the least crazy thing I've done all day."

In eighth grade, Danny's adviser at his old school noticed that he'd run up a tab of fifteen overdue library books on T. S. Eliot. At first, his teachers figured he was just a poser. Danny didn't pay attention in class and his marks were below average, so they assumed he just liked carrying them around for show. Then they asked him a few questions about *The Waste Land*. A month later, Danny was labeled "gifted" and he transferred out. Kris's favorite part of the story is that he never returned the books.

"Fair point," I said, wondering what Kris and Luke were doing right now. I couldn't stop picturing them—on a stoop, in the park, outside her townhouse. He'd probably have his fucking guitar.

Sliding my hand into my jeans pocket, I searched for my coin. It was nestled next to my school ID, and I pressed my fingers against the cool metal. I pulled it out and rubbed it softly with my thumb.

Danny stepped toward me. "Where'd you get that?"

"It was my father's." I didn't know why I'd told him the truth. Kris was the only one who knew.

"It's gold?"

"Yeah, not much, though."

"Your pops was Indiana fucking Jones." Danny pointed at the face on the coin. "Who's the guy?"

"This king, Ella-Asbeha."

"Old school?"

"Yup. The Aksumite Kingdom," I said, nodding. "Somewhere in East Africa."

"And you just carry it around with you?"

"Keeps me company." I took out my wallet and tucked the coin back in. It felt good to have Ella back where he belonged. "So I was thinking, you should probably hang back before we get to the party."

"Why's that?" Danny said anxiously.

"Who knows who'll be there? I'm sure there'll be a couple MKIIs."

Danny gnawed on his lower lip. "I guess you're right."

There are about a dozen prep schools in the city, and when a party has been brewing for a couple days, they all show up. Everybody knows everybody. Maybe they went to the same camp, or their families summered together, or they played each other in football. Then so-and-so will tell so-and-so and her boyfriend will bring a few of his buddies, and all of a sudden there's a crowd.

"There's that twenty-four-hour magazine store on Madison," Danny said, nodding west. "I could kill some time there. How long will you be?"

"No idea. I mean, not that long." I didn't know what the hell to say to Greg. I was convinced he was going to start laughing at me.

"Well, do what you gotta do. I'll go catch up on *The New Yorker.*"

We shook hands and Danny headed toward Madison.

———

"I'm gonna throw up a pair of pieces," Greg said. *"One high, one low."* He reached into his bag and came out double-fisting cans. *"Kodie, you wanna fill?"*

"I'm on it," Kodak said, putting down his second Pop-Tart.

Kodak tried writing on his own a couple times but he said the paint fucked up his breathing. We needed the backup anyway. You always need someone working fill-ins and running lookout.

"You gotta help me later," I said, switching fingers. The can was freezing my hand, but I wasn't letting go for anything. The hard edges of my D were starting to come into focus, and the glossed surface bounced the steady flashing of traffic signals onto the front of my hoodie.

A curtain of sunlight was sliding gradually down the far wall of Quik Park. We had forty minutes, maybe fifty, until sophomore assembly. Some mornings I'd pretend that Mick from Rocky was standing behind me with a stopwatch.

"Under an hour," I said, turning to Greg.

Miniature pools of paint clung to the chips and divots in the brick. From ten feet away, all you could see was the full surface color, but as you stepped closer, tiny runs and cracks splintered the characters.

———

When I turned the corner on 98th, I knew exactly where the party was. About twenty people were hanging outside the second building on the block. I recognized a bunch of West Side girls and some prep-school hoods passing a fresh blunt around.

On Saturday nights, prep-school hoods spend their time practicing their thuggish poses and their shortest, cruelest smiles. Like they're so cool they don't even know what to do with themselves. Usually if you see a whole prep-school crew, half of them will be studying the street and the other half will be saying "fuck you" with their eyes. And working so hard to own the pavement, none of them want to admit that their white asses sleep in Fifth Avenue duplexes.

Jerry Rosencrant and Adam Guild were leaning against the building drinking forties. They were both in my grade at Daley and they were real friendly with the Diggs. There weren't enough hoods at Daley to start a crew, so guys like Jerry and Adam kind of drifted around minding their own business, like Switzerland.

Jerry walked slowly over to me in his new Nautica jacket. "What up, Thet?" he said, throwing his palm out. "What you doing here, yo?"

"What's going on?" I asked, ignoring the jab.

"Nothing. It's mad hot upstairs."

"How many peeps?" I said, surprised by my own slang. I could feel my pulse skipping, just being around it all again.

"Crazy heads up in that crib," he said. "Too many West Side peeps. I've been chillin' down here smokin' blunts and shit. You wanna puff?"

Jerry loved to mess with our Spanish teacher, Madame Cisneros. She was a senile old lady known for wearing this horrible wig, and Jerry was famous for telling her that she had something on her glasses. He loved to watch her slide them back on, one side at a time, so that she didn't shift her head of hair.

"I think I'm gonna wait a bit," I said. "Hey, you seen Greg?"

"*LUST?* I think so, yo."

Adam stumbled toward us and gave Jerry a playful punch. "Wazzup, boyz?" he cackled. "Yo, someone taxed my Big Bamboos."

"Well, I think I'm gonna go check out upstairs," I said, shaking hands with Adam.

"Coolio." Jerry nodded. "We'll see you back up there. And hey, if you decide you wanna puff, we got lots of fucking herb."

The elevator doors slid open, and Ashley Burton stepped off with two friends I'd met before. They were all wearing tank tops and tight black pants, and Ashley's hair was held up in a bun by two miniature blue chopsticks. The three girls were in the grade below me, but they'd dated a couple friends of mine, and they knew they'd date a couple more.

"Nickie, sweetie, how are you?" She leaned in to kiss me. Both cheeks. "You know Stacy and Emily." Ashley was much prettier than her friends and you could see that she enjoyed that.

"Is Jenny with you?" I asked, searching for something to say. Jenny had dated Adam for most of last year.

"I don't know what's up with that girl," Ashley complained.

"Oh, my God," Emily said, laughing. "Is she the one with that clunky cell phone?"

Stacy grinned. "That thing isn't a cell phone. It's like a portable phone with good reception."

"Talk about StarTac-ky," Emily said, nodding.

"She's just changed," Ashley continued. "But people change, right, Nickie?"

"It's like you think you know somebody," I said, keeping a straight face. There's nothing more annoying than a girl whose life philosophy is based on the shape of her ass.

Ashley raised her shoulders playfully. "Well, we're out of here."

"I don't even know why we came all the way up to Ninety-eighth," Emily hissed at Ashley.

"Sara's good people," Ashley said defensively.

I nodded. "She's great."

Emily grinned. "Well, if I break Ninety-sixth Street, I feel like I should be doing community service."

Ashley kissed me on the cheek once more. "So good to see you, Nickie." She walked out of the lobby with her two friends and disappeared into the crowd.

Ashley and Kodak used to live in the same building on Fifth. Years ago, she had a habit of passing out at all the wrong times, and her girlfriends were always calling Kodak and asking him to take her home. He didn't mind because she had a tiny frame and, I guess, some attention is always better than none. Kodak wasn't a horrible-looking guy but it's not like girls were passing notes about him. One time, he showed me some of the pictures he'd taken of Ashley sleeping. When he first pulled out the binder, I braced myself for some sick shit, but they were all really beautiful portraits. Some guys would've taken advantage of her, but that just wasn't Kodak's style.

As soon as I stepped off the elevator, it was clear which apartment the party was in. A guy was sitting in the hallway with his back to the wall, resting his head in his hands. He was coming down from something, and his girlfriend was standing angrily over him, her purse slung across her shoulder. When I reached the front door, I could see the doorknob rattling in time to the stereo's bass.

I opened the door and a wave of smoke, alcohol, and body heat washed over me. People were everywhere. Every couch, chair, table, counter, desk, and rug was covered with kids. There were people hanging out in the den doing coke off compact mirrors and two couples screwing around underneath an oak dining-room table. I hadn't been to a house party like this in over a year, and I couldn't decide if I was nervous or excited or both.

I walked down the main hallway, between conversations and over a couple of passed-out freshmen. Sara's parents were rare-rug dealers, and her apartment was covered with these beautiful Oriental carpets. Nobody at the party cared. Everywhere I looked, there were stamped-out cigarette butts and kicked-over cans of cheap beer.

I checked the front rooms first. The kitchen, the library, the living room. No sign of Greg. Walking through the dining room, I tripped over a bottle of Jack Daniel's and nearly shattered my elbow on a grandfather clock. In the master bedroom, I spotted Tim in the far corner. Nancy was leaning against his chest and Tim was talking with a linebacker from Fiedler.

The linebacker had had a couple too many, but linebackers always do.

Turning back around, I headed down another hallway. The walls were decorated with dozens of elegant family photos, and I wondered if Sara's parents would still be smiling when they came back home. I tried one of the doors, but the lights were off inside and all I could hear was sloppy breathing. In the bathroom, I found three kids tearing through a case of nitrous tanks. No Greg. Where the hell was he?

A kid walked into me carrying a pair of half-eaten DoveBars. He looked up at me with a confused smile and then pressed on. At house parties, the fridge always gets raided and desserts are usually the first to go. I couldn't believe how I used to live for this shit.

I walked back into the living room and scanned the crowd for Greg's red hair. An old Dr. Dre tune came blasting out of the speakers. Next to the bookshelves, I found Adam flipping through Sara's father's collection of classical CDs.

"Adam," I yelled, hoping he wasn't a total waste. "Where's Greg?"

Adam stared up at me, pupils the size of quarters. "Schubert died mad young, yo."

"I need to talk to Greg," I said. "Jerry said he was here."

"Boy probably peaced out."

"Where'd he go? It's important."

"Important," Adam said, fighting a burp. "Shit's crazy necessary?" The burp won.

I nodded. "Can you get in touch with him? I don't have his cell anymore."

"Yo, chillz, I could find him." Adam plucked a CD from its jewel case and slid it into the back pocket of his khakis. "Give me a few."

"I'll be back," I said, annoyed. Why wasn't I sitting next to Kris at the late show, breathing in the popcorned air? Last night, I'd left Victoria's convinced that everything in my life was about to change, but I never thought that meant for the worse.

I wove my way out of the living room and headed for Tim and Nancy. I figured I'd hang with them until Adam tracked Greg down.

Tim spotted me from his corner of the bedroom. "Nick," he shouted. "What are you doing here?"

"Changed my mind," I said, shrugging it off.

He studied my eyes and tightened his grip on Nancy's shoulder. "For real?"

Leaning toward Tim, I shielded my mouth. "Danny, you know, Kris's brother? He's in trouble with these MKII kids," I said, intentionally mumbling my words. "I want to talk to Greg Carmichael about helping him out. Before MKII beats the shit out of him."

Nancy shook her head slowly. "Oh my God, Nick."

"What's wrong with those kids?" Tim lifted his beer. "They're fucking deranged."

Sara popped out of the crowd looking like she was about to burst into tears. "Tim, what the hell am I going to do?"

"Ask some people to leave," he said.

"Some of those IPO guys took all my mom's fucking jewelry," she cried.

"Those IPO guys are assholes," I muttered. "Are they still here?"

"I don't know," she groaned.

"Fuck," Tim said. "I'm sorry, Sara."

There was a thud in the other room and the sound of glass breaking. Sara turned around and looked at her apartment. "I don't know any of these people," she shouted as she dissolved back into the party. I felt for her but she was crazy to throw an all-city party.

Tim crushed his empty. "Where's IPO from?"

"Dwiggins," I said.

"What's it stand for again?"

"Ill Posse Outlaws. Or maybe it's International Posse Outlaws. I can never remember," I said, reaching for a fresh butt. "All lacrosse players, I think. Real blue-blood thugs."

"That's so strange," Nancy said. "I mean, in my town most of the screw-ups aren't, like, the rich kids and stuff."

"Manhattan's funny like that," Tim declared.

"That's an understatement," I agreed.

Prep-school hoods could only exist in a city like New York. Take the average pissed-off teenage guy, add a platinum card and workaholic parents, and put him in a city where every drink, drug, and weapon can be delivered within the hour, and there's a good chance he'll end up like Greg or Derrick. Suburban kids just don't have the toys.

Nancy tugged on Tim's sweater. "Baby, I'm going to go use the powder room. Okay?"

"Do you want me to go with you?" Tim asked.

Nancy smiled at me. "I'm a big girl, guys." She placed a kiss on Tim's cheek and made her way out of the bedroom.

A kid from Daley walked by with a case of Natty Light, and Tim grabbed two. "So, Kris asked you to help out her brother?"

he said, tossing me a beer. "'Cause you used to know these sorts of kids."

"Not really. I mean, I just bumped into Danny after I left you guys. So I figured . . ."

"Huh." Tim flexed the tab of his beer until it gave. "This girl's got her hooks into you pretty deep, Nick."

"This isn't just about Kris," I said, brushing it off. I'd never talked to Tim about that night and Kodak. I guess I'd never really talked to anyone about it. "Besides, I'm just as hooked on her."

Tim laughed. "That's what I meant."

I took a slug of my beer. "What about you? Shit with Nancy looks good." Tim never said it outright, but I could tell he was pretty taken with Nancy. And standing there pissed off at Luke and Kris and everything else that was fucking up my weekend, I understood why.

"Good. I guess," Tim said, pausing.

"What is it?"

"Real confidential," he said, lowering his voice.

"Done."

"Well, I know this is ridiculous but *it* makes me nervous."

"What do you mean *it*?"

Tim leaned toward me. "I mean *it*."

"Oh," I said, trying not to look surprised. Last week, he'd mentioned that they were talking about sleeping together. "*It's* supposed to make you nervous."

Tim always jokes that he's a V-card gold member since birth and we used to all agree that Tim had "the curse." For the first two years of high school, every time he'd make a move on a girl, something would go wrong. February of sophomore year his cab got a flat tire going across the Brooklyn Bridge. He had to stand outside in the snow apologizing to this Andrews girl who never spoke to him again. Twice during junior year his date passed out while they were kissing; once he did. The worst was at the beginning of the summer when Anne Gough's mother walked in on them sixty-nining on the kitchen floor at two in the morning. She screamed so loudly that the neighbors called the cops. Mrs. Gough thought there was a dead guy in the kitchen.

"Have you ever taken a really good look at *it?*" Tim asked, and burped.

"At what?" Tim wasn't talking about sex.

"At *it.* Like really up close?"

"Depends," I said. "I guess, sort of. But usually I don't stop and stare."

"No, I'm not saying I stop and stare. But you can't help but take a good look. And that's when I get a little wigged-out."

"Well, I'm sure she's just as nervous when she's dealing with you," I said, trying to reassure him.

"I don't think so. She seems to know what she's doing."

"Are you quick?" I said, grinning. That's what I loved about Tim. No matter how stressed I was, he'd always have me laughing within five minutes.

He blushed. "Yeah."

"How quick?"

"I don't know."

"Could you make it through the 'Star-Spangled Banner'?" I smiled.

"Who's singing?" Tim laughed.

Adam hollered to me from across the room. He'd stripped

down to his wife-beater and he was carrying a skinny Nokia in his raised palm, like a five-star waiter. "Thet," Adam shouted. "I gots Carmichaels for you."

Tim slapped me on the back. "Good luck, kid."

Adam passed me the phone and then leaned up against the wall with a satisfied smile on his face. He was five minutes away from yelling at the carpet.

Pressing the phone to my chest, I scanned the room for a quiet place to talk. I couldn't say what I needed to in front of Adam and Tim and everybody else at the party. I wasn't even sure I could say it in the first place.

I made my way back out into the hallway and searched for an empty bathroom. A few steps from the living room, I found a closet that nobody seemed to be using. Pushing aside a rack of overcoats, I stepped inside and closed the door. It had to be ninety degrees inside the closet, but the sound of the party was cut in half.

I stood there for a few seconds and tried to pull my shit together. What the hell was I doing? For nearly two years I'd been pushing Greg away, rehashing excuses, blocking—now I was about to ask for a fucking favor.

"Greg, it's Nick." My voice was steady.

"Wazzup? You miss me?"

"I got a little bit of a problem."

"Yo, you gots to speak up, I'm in a cab with Julie and Tyler," he yelled.

"I got a problem," I repeated.

"What? Where you at, yo?"

"I'm at Sara's party."

"That place is whacked. We bailed a while ago."

"Greg, is anything new with MKII?" My fingers were trembling and I grabbed the closet doorknob. What was I so afraid of?

"They dropped that baller from Freid. Smashed his nose in. One sec ... Nah, we'll be theres in a minute ... Yeah, Nick ... In two minutes, chill ... Nick? And I think they're after some head who got nice with Derrick's girl, but I don't know what that shit's about."

"The kid they're looking for is Kris's brother."

"Your Kris? Well, he better hide. Get scarce, kid ... Don't smoke all that ... And Nick, don't be chilling with this dude when they find him. MKII's crazy indiscriminate like that."

"They already popped him once," I said. "What can we do?"

"With guys like that, there's not much," Greg said, inhaling. "Derrick's mad twisted."

"Any more than the rest?"

"Definitely. My boy keeps rats. Like as pets and shit."

"What? How the fuck does he do that?"

"Keeps'm in a cage on his roof. He's always feeding them pigeons and shit. I've seen it. It's fucking sick."

The closet door shuddered as somebody leaned their date against it. "So he's out of his fucking mind," I whispered. Danny was a dead man.

"Yup," Greg wheezed, holding in a hit. "Boy's real antisocial, but he runs a tight crew."

"There's gotta be something we can do."

"Something *we* can do?" Greg laughed. "I was thinking about what *you* could do, Nick."

"Is that how it is?" I said, trying not to raise my voice.

"That's how your ass wanted it last time I checked."

I kneeled down below the suits. "And there's nothing to be said for old friends?"

"Am I talking to Nick or Thet?"

"What?" I stammered. This was humiliating.

"Nick or Thet?"

"Both." I knew Greg was tooling on me, but I couldn't watch another friend of mine go down. Not Danny.

"Fuck that. Neither."

I leaned my forehead against a rack of boots. "Thet," I said, tensing my chest. "At least for now."

"My brother," Greg cried.

The closet didn't spin me around like Clark Kent, but something changed. Instead of going home, watching the late movie, and jerking off, I was suddenly committed.

"I'll need to set up a meeting with'm," Greg said. "I'm sure Derrick won't want to give up the manhunt, but I can spin my diplomacy vibes."

At Collier, Greg loved to think he took care of me. When we got busted smoking a joint on the stoop outside school, when a liquor store called the cops on my fake ID, Greg always wanted to take the hit. It made him feel important.

"How soon?" I asked.

"Sooner's always better. If we want this shit dealt with humanely."

"Name the spot."

"Okay, you know a head named Jeremy Prescott? Tall peep from Troy, always eating cherry Pez. Been a Dignitary about a year."

"I've heard his name before," I said.

"He lives on Fieldston Road in Riverdale. His parents are gone for a while, so we'll all be chillin' there later. He's got a choice house, so shit's real laid-back."

"All right."

"And call my celly when you get to the Two hundred forty-second Street station." I reached into my jeans for a pen and wrote the number on my wrist. "I'll have some peeps come and pick you up."

"We'll be there ASAP."

"What's your celly?" Greg exhaled.

"I don't have one," I said, bracing myself for Greg's comment. Kris and I both agreed they were more trouble than they were worth. Besides, half the calls would be from Elliot.

"You're still Mr. Black-and-White Movies Guy, huh?" Greg laughed.

"I guess you could say that," I muttered.

"Well, lose those loafers."

"Uh-huh," I said, squeezing the cell. I felt like telling him to go fuck himself, but I'd promised Danny. Greg loved this.

"And Thet."

"Yeah?"

"Welcome home." *Beep.*

———

I lifted Kodak's Nikon to my eye and measured the frame. I didn't want any of the cars in the picture but there was no way around it. The piece had a six-foot wingspan and it stretched over the hoods of two 7-Series.

"Take the fucking picture already, Thet," Greg said, picking up his backpack.

I held my breath and pressed the shutter. Sliding the lens cover onto the camera, I handed it back to Kodak. I had to document every piece, especially a fresh style. That way, if some toy came along and crossed me out, at least I'd have a record.

I pulled my hoodie over my shoulders and let it fall to the ground. A young woman jogged by in spandex and a Chase Manhattan T-shirt. Before I could think to hide, she was gone. She wasn't going to call the cops, though. Most New Yorkers don't give a shit.

"Five-O?" Kodak said, searching Greg and me for an answer.

"Nah," I mumbled.

I nearly freaked out the first time we got busted, but the cops always had a sense of humor about the whole thing. They'd usually line us up against the wall and spray our backs and hair and pants with our own paint. They never dragged us in.

Greg laughed. "Yo, that bitch saw you naked."

I looked down at my bare chest and smiled. "Probably made her morning," I said, grinning.

I emptied the laundry bag onto the concrete and searched for my oxford. My blazer was completely wrinkled but I didn't give a shit. The only thing my teachers ever noticed was the paint on my fingers. I'd spend ten minutes scrubbing my hands at McDonald's, but I could never get rid of it all.

———

I hung up Adam's cell. I needed a drink. Fast. I swung the closet door open, and it jerked to a stop halfway through its arc.

"Motherfucker!" a voice yelled.

The door flew all the way open and a guy stared in at me. He had slicked curly black hair and his dark leather belt held up a sagging pair of khakis. "What the fuck do we have here?" he shouted.

Maybe it was the head rush from standing up so quickly, or the combo of Jameson and cheap beer, but I didn't recognize Derrick until he gripped my shoulder. My stomach clenched.

"Yo, you one of them crazy public places perverts?"

The hallway bulbs seemed to be throwing off twice as much light as before. What the fuck could I do? "Sorry about that," I said, as casually as I could.

Another hood showed up behind Derrick and started sizing me up.

"As a guest," Derrick sneered, "you shouldn't go around getting nice with yourself in other people's closets."

"Sorry, I—"

"Sorry?" Derrick leaned into me, hard. His nose had been broken so many times that it zigzagged its way down toward the bow of his upper lip. "Your bitch ass is a public nuisance, and all you can say is, 'Sorry'?"

I had no idea what to do if he swung at me. A pellet of sweat took off down my forehead and scalded my left eye.

"Derrick," a girl yelled from down the hall. She had long blond hair and she looked furious at somebody. "I'm out of here."

"Jessica," Derrick shouted, stepping past me. All I could think was *way to go, Danny,* and then he was gone. I'd barely said a word to Derrick and I hated him already.

"You got off mad easy." Derrick's friend laughed and squared off with me. "Domestic disputes and shit."

"I didn't mean to—"

Out of nowhere, Jerry threw his hand on the kid's back. "Chillz," Jerry said, drunkenly. "Nick's good peoples."

"Yo, I don't know about that." The hood looked me up and down, then shifted his glance to Jerry. Without saying another word, he turned and walked slowly back toward the living room.

"What the fuck is up with those guys?" I said.

Jerry smiled. "That kid's crazy as fucking shit. He's smoked, yo."

Jerry's cell phone chirped. "S'up? S'up?" he shouted. Then his intonation flattened. "Mother, where are you calling me from?" He signaled to me that he'd need a minute and then cupped his hand over the phone. "No, of course I understand. . . . It's just that I tried on those. . . . No, we're going to play pool." He leaned his head back and mimed a scream. "I know it's a special occasion," he whispered. "Okay . . . yes . . . I gotta go . . . Gotta go," he said, slamming his cell phone shut. He turned to me and took out a pocket-sized bottle of Visine. "This place is whacked."

I walked back into the bedroom and took two long, full breaths. Why was I such a pussy? I couldn't even handle talking to Derrick. This whole weekend was collapsing—I could feel it.

I handed Adam his cell and used whatever cool I had left. "Thanks, Adam. I owe you one."

"Chilz, yo," Adam said, grinning. "Anything for the great Thet."

"There's a kid bleeding in the bathroom," Tim said anxiously. "He scared Nancy."

Nancy was blotting her sweater with a wet paper towel.

She'd obviously collided with someone and ended up wearing half their drink. "I think we should leave," she whispered.

"Yeah." Tim took Nancy's hand and looked over at me.

The three of us weaved our way out into the hallway, saying random good-byes and trying not to step on anybody. There was a line for the elevator, but I was just glad to be out of the apartment.

Downstairs, a crowd was gathering on the sidewalk. Nobody wanted to be inside the building when the cops arrived. Sometimes the police would show up because there were fifty kids hanging outside a building; other times the neighbors would call them, and once in a while the person throwing the party would do it, just to put a stop to the evening. But everybody knew they'd be here sooner or later.

"It looks like it's clearing out," Nancy said.

"Yeah, the doorman across the street called the cops," Tim said. "At least that's the buzz."

I lit a cigarette and took a long drag. "Let's get out of here."

As we turned to walk toward Park, Sara threw open the door to her building and started screaming down the street at the group of ten or so hoods who were hanging out down the block. She'd started crying, and her face and eyes were swollen.

"Is that IPO?" Nancy asked.

"Yeah," I said. I could tell just by looking at them.

"You fucking assholes," Sara yelled.

Two guys in IPO stopped Sara from walking toward the rest of their crew and one of them leaned over and said something in her ear. The heads of IPO didn't even turn to look at her. Most prep-school crews have one or two leaders, and a practiced eye can tell who they are instantly. To run a crew like IPO, you don't have to be the richest or the strongest or the loudest. You just need to be ready to risk more than anybody else will. Whether it's stealing or fucking, drinking or fighting, tagging or dosing, you never back down.

"I won't shut up," Sara cried. "You guys are going to get me in so much fucking trouble."

Sara rushed toward IPO, and this time the two hoods pushed her back. She stumbled a little, and the taller guy raised his hand to tell her to back off. A couple IPO hoods looked over at Sara and laughed. They were bastards, and they were proud of it.

"You guys are assholes," she screamed. "I'm calling the cops."

Two of Sara's girlfriends tried to grab hold of her wrist, but she brushed them off. Sara turned her back on IPO and started to walk toward her building.

"I'm glad that's over," Nancy said.

After a couple steps, Sara pivoted and charged back at IPO. She ran by the two guys who'd stopped her before and shoved one of the leaders in the back.

I didn't see it coming. I don't think any of the hoods in IPO did either. But the guy Sara shoved spun around on his right boot, arm extended, palm open, and smacked her across the side of her face. It sounded like a firecracker. Sara's head swung back, and her knees buckled forward onto the pavement. The guy stood over her for a moment, smiling at the silence he'd created. Then IPO took off in a dead sprint across 98th Street toward the river, their hoods flapping behind them.

Two of Sara's friends helped her up and then walked her back inside. My legs were shaking. What the fuck was IPO trying to prove? Half of me felt like chasing after them, and the other part of me just wanted to sit down on the pavement and cry. My hand scrambled into my pocket and dug around for my coin. Ella had fallen out of my wallet and I brushed some tobacco off his face. I needed something to hold on to.

Across the street, a group of adults was starting to gather and the doormen from the neighboring buildings were all standing in the road. Nancy's face was buried in Tim's shoulder. Everything felt so fucking wrong.

I walked with Tim and Nancy to the corner. Three cop cars blazed by us with their sirens groaning and lights spinning, and I stood there trying to slow my pulse with deep breaths.

"We're going back to my place. I've had enough of this shit," Tim said, flagging a cab. "You want us to drop you off?"

"I've got to meet up with Danny." I felt like going home and hiding underneath my comforter, but Greg had said "Yes." I still couldn't believe he was going to help us.

"All right." Tim nodded. "I want my boy to stay out of trouble."

"I'll tell him you said that."

"I was talking about you, Nick."

———

My eyes slid halfway open and I passed the joint to this cute field hockey player who I'd just met. We'd been introduced when Greg, Kodak, and I arrived at the house party, and I'd spent the last hour telling her about the Quik Park pieces we'd finished that morning. Everybody at the party was talking about them.

"That's a crazy story, Thet," the girl said, tickling the back of my neck.

"Yeah." Neon triangles were dancing with each other on the back of my eyelids, like a slow-motion screen saver. "It was a good morning." I couldn't remember whose apartment it was, but the place was soaked in Phillies blunts and rookie cleavage, and the parents were anywhere else but home.

Greg walked over to my couch and tossed me his cell. "Kodak wants you." Kodak had gone downstairs to try and line up a fifty-bag.

I lifted the phone to my ear. "S'up? Where you at?"

"Thet, let's roll," Kodak shouted. "I just made a date with an eighth of an ounce, and we got enough Andrew Jacksons to wipe out a reservation."

"I need a few," I said, looking over at the field hockey player. She smiled and rolled her eyes at me. She had the kind of smile that could make any guy forget his own name.

"Thet, I'm talking hydroponic buds," Kodak cried.

"You wanna bust?" I asked Greg.

Greg nodded. If Greg had a girl on the hook he wouldn't leave a burning building, and I was supposed to just walk. Fuck it.

I pressed the StarTAC to my cheek. "Kodie, I'll be downstairs in five." I snapped the phone closed.

"See you outside," Greg said, stomping toward the front door.

The field hockey player tossed her Marlboro Lights into her purse. "It was nice—"

"I've just gotta run an errand," I said apologetically.

"Uh-huh." She sighed.

"Will you be here in a half-hour?"

"Maybe," she said, running her fingertips down my shoulder. "But I'm here now."

I knew I was real high and I knew it was real late, but she was wearing this sparkling lip gloss, and when you're a baked sophomore, *that can feel like the prettiest thing you've ever seen. Brushing away her bangs, I leaned toward her. Our kiss tasted like Captain Morgan's and Diet Coke, and her breasts pressed against my chest. People swam around us, but I didn't give a shit.*

———

I found Danny in the back aisle of Global News. He was reading a folded copy of *Time* magazine and gnawing on a pack of Twizzlers. From the look of the store clerk, he hadn't paid for either yet.

"Danny," I said, tapping his magazine. "We're going to the Bronx." I ripped a Twizzler from his pack. "Greg's gonna set up a meeting with MKII so you can settle this."

"That's great," Danny said, beaming. "Thank you, Nick."

I wasn't proud of my past, but it felt good to hear. I just couldn't decide if it was worth dredging everything back up.

"Why would Greg do that for me?" Danny stuffed the magazine into its plastic cubby.

"He wouldn't. He's doing it to prove something to me."

"What's that?"

"That I made a mistake a long time ago," I said.

"Did you?"

"Yeah, but not the one he thinks. I gotta stop off at home and grab some more money."

"Can you spot me?" Danny asked, grinning. "You wouldn't believe the markup on licorice."

I paid for the candy and we started back to Elliot's place. Danny spent the walk hollowing out strands of Twizzlers and turning them into soggy whistles.

"I ran into your friend, Derrick," I said. "I mean, literally."

"What?" Danny cried. "He was at the party?"

"Yup. Him and your girl. I thought he was going to drop me for bumping into him."

"What a mess," Danny said, raising his palms to the sky. "You know, I can't stop thinking about how fucking clichéd this whole thing is. The girl, being chased by this gang. I mean, it's a dime-store novel, for god's sake."

"But it gets updated. There's a reason *Footloose* was a hit decades after *Rebel Without a Cause*."

"Of course," Danny declared. "But don't you see why hoods are so obsolete? Guys like Greg and Derrick might have made sense in the thirties or fifties, but now everything's digital, wireless, ones and zeros." He flicked the antenna of a Grand Cherokee. "I mean, these hoods have all this fucking anger and adrenaline, and they could do so much more than smash heads and smoke blunts. It's such a meaningless way to deal with shit."

"So what should hoods do instead?" I asked. "Start book clubs?"

Danny laughed. "You really want to know?"

"Sure," I said, stepping over a pile of cardboard boxes that someone had thrown away.

"All right. I decided tonight that I want to start a movement. One of those intellectual jobs like modernism and postmodernism."

"Okay." I spent a week once watching Antonioni films, but I never figured out how to explain modernism. "What are you going to call yours?"

"Drumroll please," Danny said, smiling. "Conformism. With a capital C. See the whole idea is that you do exactly what you think you're supposed to do. I mean, it's the logical inversion of the rebel, the hood."

I looked over at Danny to see if he was serious. Kris was always telling me about her brother's newest theory, but he'd never pitched me before. "So instead of hoods, you want kids who do their homework and say all the right shit at cocktail parties."

"Yeah, but not because they're spineless dorks," Danny said. "See, Conformists will do their homework because they know that going to a good college will give them more power, more access. It's just a matter of rechanneling that anger until you can actually have some influence."

"So you can end up some stockbroker or real estate guy? I'm not interested."

"No, so you can end up a public defender or a journalist. Fuck it, so you can end up a congressman. People like that matter."

"You're still part of the whole system," I said dismissively. Before my father left on a trip, he would always remind me that he went to work in sandals and a T-shirt. He loved reading Thoreau and there was one quote that he had sewn into a throw pillow: "I say beware of all enterprises that require new clothes." My father never understood how people could wear a tie every day.

"But you need to be part of the system these days," Danny said. "To some degree at least. Otherwise, you might as well be smoking herb in Central Park with MKII."

I shrugged my shoulders. "But why would anybody ever pay attention to these Conformists?"

"That's exactly why they're perfect. They're not the wild ones. They can get inside, understand shit, and fix it. They're conforming to be Conformists."

Turning off Lexington, we walked past a line of brownstones and city elms, and headed toward Park. Each house was four or five stories high, and they were built in every style. On one night or another, Kris and I had sat on the steps of every one of those brownstones.

"So you want everyone to brownnose their way through high school?"

"Sure, there's some brownnosing involved." Danny nodded. "But you're not selling out. It's more like selling in."

"And who would want to be a Conformist?"

"Somebody just like you, Nick."

"What are you talking about?" I said. "Why not you?"

"When you get sent to rehab at fourteen, the CIA starts a file on you. Besides, I've been having a little trouble with authority these days."

"What kind of benefits are you offering?" I asked. "Dental and—"

"Fuck."

I looked over at Danny. His face was completely pale. "What?"

He nodded down the block toward Elliot's awning. "Tell me those are friends of yours."

Four hoods were leaning against a blue BMW parked outside Elliot's building. A built kid in Double RL noticed that we'd stopped walking and took a step toward Danny and me. His friends took their hands out of their jackets and followed behind him. When they hit the light from the awning, I saw their grinning faces and slanted baseball caps.

I took a step back. "Can you—"

"Like the Road Runner," Danny finished.

"Stay by me," I said, taking another step.

"You stay by me," he said, turning around.

And then we bolted. We sprinted back around the corner toward Lexington.

"FUCKING HERBS!"

Danny ran in front of me down the side street and I knocked trash cans over behind us. Two couples turned the corner on Lexington and nearly clotheslined Danny. He jumped onto the hood of a parked Saab and leapt into 75th Street. A Ranger screeched to a stop in front of him and I sprang off the Saab, onto the hood of the Ranger, and then onto the other side of the block.

"Oh, Danny boy," a voice sang out.

Danny and I spun around the corner onto Lexington, shoes squeaking behind us, and collided with a woman walking her five dogs. Danny hit the leashes full force and tripped into a broken parking meter. I bounced off the metal shutters of a shoe store and fell into a lab that was pretty happy to have someone to play with. Leaping over the rest of the leashes, I grabbed Danny by the collar and pushed him forward.

The dogs started barking again when the hoods turned the corner and I pointed toward the bodega in the middle of the block.

"Come on," I said, running down the aisle of the outdoor display and into a woman carrying two boxes of paper towels. I rolled off of her and knocked over a bed of ice and Florida grapefruits. One of the hoods grabbed my sleeve and threw a punch into my back. Tripping into the bodega, I slid across the linoleum and crashed into the cashier's counter. My hands broke the fall and I could feel scalding scratches on my palms and fingers. Two middle-aged guys carrying cases of Milwaukee's Best and Fritos stared down at me.

"Officer Zucker!" I shouted up to the two guys. I didn't know what else to do.

The Double RL hood froze at the door to the bodega and his three friends appeared behind him.

"Officers—" I gasped again.

The guy holding the Fritos studied my ice-covered face and my bleeding hand. The hoods smiled at each other.

"Son," he said, shaking his head, "you're always playing too rough." Then he turned to the hoods still perched at the door. "Get on home, boys."

They laughed and turned back to the sidewalk. "Later, pussies," one of them shouted. "You're mine, Thet."

I dropped my head to the cold, red tiles of the bodega and felt my bruised rib.

"Are you okay?"

This was fucking bullshit. I didn't care if MKII wanted to play cops'n robbers all around New York City, but leave me the hell out of it.

"Are you okay?" the other guy asked again. "Do you need—"

"I'm fine," I said, standing up. "Thank you, guys."

They nodded and slammed their beer on the counter. "You know, I thought about applying for the academy."

Danny walked up from the back of the bodega and put his hand on my shoulder. "Thanks for grabbing me back there."

"No problem. Were those Conformists?" I asked, holding my hand to my side.

Danny sneered and rubbed his forehead against his shirt-sleeve. "How the hell did they know where I was?"

"Jerry," I wheezed. After I left Sara's party, Jerry probably told Derrick's friend that I used to write *DOA,* that I was in his Spanish class at Daley, that I was best friends with Kris Conway.

"What the hell are we gonna do?" Danny asked.

I didn't know who else to call. "Can I use the phone?" I asked the store clerk.

He slid it toward me and I punched in Greg's cell. It rang once.

"It's Nick."

"I'm sorry, sir," Greg said, in his most professional tone. "I don't know a Nick."

"Greg, we just got jumped outside my building. They were fucking waiting for me," I said, trying not to sound freaked out.

"What?" Greg shouted. "Why the fuck would MKII track you?"

"I—"

"Wait," Greg interrupted. "Where you at? I'm sending some boyz there."

"Greg, you—"

"Thet, give me your fucking digits."

"Seventy-fifth and Lex," I said. "In the bodega halfway down the block."

"Coolio. It shouldn't take these heads that long. Wait for them and then get the hell up to Riverdale."

"Did you talk to Derrick?"

"For a sec. They won't mess with you guys if you're rolling with Diggs. Shit's a cease-fire."

"Thanks."

"No worries." Greg laughed. "I always liked protecting your ass." *Beep.*

I hung up the phone and studied the cut on my hand. The

scrape ran across my palm and onto my wrist, and it stung like crazy. "Greg's sending a bunch of guys."

I grabbed a stack of napkins off the counter and pressed them against my cut. I was a wreck. Walking to Kris's last night, there'd been one thing on my mind, and now I had a million fucking problems to deal with.

An elderly woman picked up her brown paper bag. "You boys need better goals."

"I want to go to film school," I said, holding the napkins against my hand. "I swear."

———

A tremor ran through the field hockey player's right leg, and I felt a beeper in her jeans pocket. I pulled away from our kiss—my eyes struggled open. I had no idea how long we'd been kissing.

"It's my friends," she said, checking her pager. "I'm supposed to meet them."

"Oh, shit." I looked at my watch. "I've got to go downstairs for a sec."

"All right." She kissed me on the cheek and reached for her purse. "I'm going to go find a phone."

As soon as I stepped out onto Central Park West, I knew something was wrong. Hoods were piling into the street and stopping traffic. Car horns were barking at each other. I noticed a group circling the park side of the street, but I didn't have a clue where Greg and Kodak were.

I walked in between two parked cars and headed for the crowd. A girl ran away from the group, crying into her cell phone, and bumped

*into me. I caught her as she fell. She looked up at me. "Call the cops,"
she gasped.*

*I stepped past her and sprinted across the street toward the crowd.
I shoved my way to the center of the circle.*

*Kodak was pressed up against the body of a taxi. Two hoods I'd
never seen before slammed his forehead into the windshield—I froze.
Greg grabbed one of them by the collar, but three other hoods threw
him to the ground and smacked their Timberlands into his side.
Greg's body convulsed, and he curled into a ball of obscenities.*

*I tried to shout something but my throat clenched. Stomach acid
burned the roof of my mouth. I couldn't move. What the fuck was
wrong with me?*

———

Danny waited in Elliot's lobby with three Diggs while I ran upstairs. I turned the doorknob to the apartment as quietly as I
could and pushed the door open. If I turned the knob just right,
the metal piece didn't click and then I just had to pray the hinges
didn't squeak.

I tiptoed down the hall but they spotted me from the living room. Elliot. My mother. Mr. Roberts. Mrs. Roberts. Mrs.
Roberts's dog, Dee-Dee. They were all dressed like they'd been
out on the town, and there was a half-empty bottle of Chivas on
the table. Bad sign.

"Nicholas," Mrs. Roberts said, standing up and walking over
to me for a kiss.

"Hi, Mrs. Roberts." I stuffed the bloody napkins in my back
pocket. I felt like sprinting into my room.

"Hey, your voice is still getting deeper," Mrs. Roberts said, smiling. "Isn't it, Michael?"

Mr. Roberts laughed. "Leave the poor boy alone."

I reached over and used my left hand to shake hands with Mr. Roberts.

My mother stood up and looked at my clothes. "You need a shower. Really, Nick, this is embarrassing."

"I know," I said, pretending to give a shit.

"Sit down for a second, Nick," Mr. Roberts said.

"I'm exhausted." I had to get out of there.

"Give us a second," Elliot began. "He's so busy these days." He tossed Mrs. Roberts a large wink.

"I really—"

"Nicholas," my mother interrupted. She gestured toward the empty seat.

"Let me just wash up and I'll be right back," I said, edging toward my room.

Elliot laughed. "He's harder to get on the phone than my lawyer."

I locked my door and ran over to the closet. Falling to my knees, I threw all of my old shoes into the middle of the room and then rolled two ten-pound weights to the side. I felt for the back edge of my rug and grabbed at the loose strands. Tugging at the seams of the rug, I searched for the loose floorboard. It rattled in place and I got a splinter prying it off the floor. I threw my arm into the hole and pulled out my black backpack. It was covered in dust but I could still read all our tags inked on the canvas. I tossed everything back into the closet, slammed the door, and ran into the bathroom.

I brushed the dust into the bathtub and unzipped the back-pack. The unmistakable odor of Krylon slapped my sinuses and, for a second, I felt like I was writing again. Everything was still there. I didn't know where I thought it would go, but I had to be sure. My trusty CD player that had taken more hits than I had. A cheap bowl that I'd scraped the resin out of. A couple of fat-tip markers that had probably dried out a long time ago. Two cans of Krylon and a handful of spray caps. My beaten-up red Yankees cap that had been through everything with me.

I kicked off my loafers and found my Timberlands. They were scratched up but they were the best I had. I grabbed an old hooded sweatshirt and threw it on, and then ran over to my desk and pocketed about two hundred dollars in cash. On the phone, Greg had asked me who he was talking to and I'd told him what he wanted to hear, but standing there in my old boots, I remembered what it actually felt like to be Thet. Thet, the artist who could get up on any wall or highway for miles. Thet, the sophomore who girls always wanted to meet. Thet, the guy who failed his friends.

I dropped my backpack against the front door and walked casually back into the living room. I was nervous they were going to notice my change of clothes, but they were pretty toasted.

"Good night?" Elliot said. "You had fun I trust?"

I sat down on the couch next to Mrs. Roberts. "Yeah." I nodded. Not that Elliot really cared.

"So I hear you might be working in finance this summer," Mr. Roberts said.

"I'm not sure yet." I felt like telling Mr. Roberts that I'd rather clean a Wall Street office than work in one, but I was polite. Danny would've been proud.

"I can't imagine having those opportunities when I was your age. I think I would've jumped out of my seat," Mr. Roberts said. "You'll really get to see what goes on."

"Well, we'll see," I said, trying to sit on my hand.

"So, how's Daley?" Mrs. Roberts asked. Dee-Dee was curled around the leg of her chair.

"It's fine."

"Ben's loving it these days," Mrs. Roberts said. Their son was a junior.

"That's great," I said. Their son was a fucking tool.

"You've started the big college search?" Mr. Roberts asked.

"A bit. Applications aren't due for a while."

"Well, you must've taken the SATs," Mrs. Roberts said.

"He got a fourteen-twenty," my mother said, smiling.

"Wow."

"Elliot, let Nick have a drink with us," Mrs. Roberts declared. "He's old enough."

Elliot looked to my mother for the nod. My mother paused, then gave it.

"Fourteen-ten, you said?" Mr. Roberts asked.

Elliot walked over and picked out another crystal highball glass. He poured me a double and refilled Mrs. Roberts's.

"That's a great score." Mrs. Roberts reached into her cigarette case and picked up her engraved lighter. She was the only one of my parents' friends who smoked, and I liked her for it.

"That's where Ben's hoping to score, too."

"We were very pleased," my mother said.

"You could go to your father's alma mater with a score like that," Mrs. Roberts said, sipping her drink. "You loved Princeton, didn't you, Elliot?"

"My father didn't go to college," I said, picking up the scotch and throwing it back in one long gulp.

Mrs. Roberts's drink hung in midair. I reached down to her cigarette case and pulled out a Dunhill. Standing up, I lit the cigarette and then walked out—it felt fucking great. The only noise I heard as I slammed the door shut was Dee-Dee barking.

In the lobby, Danny was swapping stories with the Diggs. I'd met the two older hoods at a party in Southampton last year, but the young guy was a shiny recruit.

"You guys mind escorting us to the subway?" I said, tossing on my Yankees hat.

The three Diggs nodded.

Danny smiled at my new outfit. "I barely recognized you."

"Shut up," I muttered, walking outside. I knew I'd have to face Elliot and my mother eventually, but I just didn't give a shit.

———

There were five people waiting on the uptown platform, including a couple leaning up against the tiled wall sharing a box of Dunkin' Donuts.

"You should call your sister and let her know where she can find us," I said. "She'll need to call a cab when she gets off the train. I mean, if she's even free," I added, as naturally as I could. I wasn't sure I could handle seeing Kris right now.

Danny walked over to a pay phone, and I sat down on an

empty wooden bench. A stale breeze sped through the station and sent ripples across the dark puddles spotting the train tracks. The train was coming. In New York City, you can smell the train before you can see it.

Danny sat down next to me and shoved his hands in his pockets. "I left her a message."

"So how's school been since you got back?" I asked, trying to skip over Kris and Luke.

"Not bad. I'm still on probation." Danny leaned back against the bench. "Which kind of sucks. What about you?"

"Up and down. I've got to write this five-pager on germanium for Monday."

The approaching train rattled the metal signs in the station and spread light across the tracks.

Danny stood up. "The semiconductor?"

"Yeah," I said, surprised.

"You know the great story behind it, right?"

The fourth car screeched to a stop in front of us, and the doors slid open. We stepped onto the subway, and Danny and I sat in two seats facing each other. There were a dozen people scattered around the car, but I didn't make eye contact with anyone.

"For real?" I asked, staring at an ad for acne treatment. The train smelled like damp newspaper.

"I swear. When Mendeleyev created the periodic table, he knew about germanium before it was ever, quote, 'discovered.' Hell, he knew stuff about germanium before anyone had ever set eyes on it. Isn't that weird?"

"How could he do something like that?"

"It's hard to explain. It's like since he knew there was a plain donut," Danny said, nodding to the couple at the other end of the car, "and a chocolate glazed, he knew there had to be a plain glazed. It just had to exist, even though he'd never eaten one. It's kind of spiritual that way."

"How do you figure?"

"Well, to believe there's this piece holding all the other elements together. To believe without actual proof."

"Do you believe in God, Danny?"

"I don't know," he said, smiling. "I believe in Bruce Springsteen, though."

"Come on. I figured you for a theory."

"I go back and forth. I'm all over the place. Descartes never counted on manic-depressives." Danny laughed. "What about you?"

I shrugged. "There's no God on Park Avenue."

The train rattled down the tracks, revealing sleeping buildings and abandoned parking lots. A little after 1:00 A.M., the subway came to a slow, skidding stop. The moon had been running alongside the train since we touched the Hudson, and now the soft, blue light wrapped itself around a sign that said WELCOME TO RIVERDALE.

Danny and I walked the platform of the elevated station and headed down a metal staircase. Stepping onto Broadway, I found a string of beaten-up pay phones. Greg's cell went straight to voicemail, and I left him a short message saying we were at the station.

Danny sat down on the first step of the staircase, and I reached for a cigarette.

Fieldston Road was the Beverly Hills of the Bronx. Sitting between Westchester and the projects, the only thing urban about Fieldston was the street numbers. Otherwise, Fieldston was about tight lawns and SUVs with all the toppings. The Diggs went to the largest of the three prep schools in the area, Melville, but they spent all their time in Manhattan. Prep-school hoods wouldn't be anything more than bait in the rest of the Bronx.

By the time I was halfway through my butt, I heard the distinct whine of a bike engine. Two yellow motorcycles rode down the hill toward us. The front bike seemed to wobble in between bursts of speed, but the back one rode comfortably through the angles.

Danny stood up and walked over to me. "Who are those guys?"

The first bike skidded up to the curb in front of us. It was a bright yellow Ducati. The frame extended awkwardly into the body of the bike but it looked like it weighed less than I did. The front rider took off his helmet, brushed his shaggy hair from his forehead, and nodded to us both.

"S'up. I'm Dave," he said, extending a hand. "You Thet?"

"Yeah," I said without hesitating. "Nice bike. Yours?"

"It's the Prescotts'," Dave said, softly tapping the handlebars. "Ducatis are crazy temperamental. They're chill in the Hamptons, but that's it."

"I'm kinda partial to four wheels," Danny said.

"This is Jarvis." Dave tipped his head as the second Ducati pulled up. "He's my Brit cousin, but he likes NYC. Boy'll hustle you out of your fucking dice and give you a new accent."

Jarvis gave a lopsided grin.

"Thanks for picking us up," I said, trying to figure out how Danny and I were going to fit safely on the two Ducatis. Whatever. It was too late to start worrying about shit like that.

When Danny and I were set, we flew up the Riverdale hill. I thought we were going to tip over coming around 243rd, but Dave didn't even flinch. He was too numb to be scared. Dave had the glossy-eyed look of a kid who's been partying so long he thinks he'll never have to go home again. A few minutes later, we pulled onto a narrow road that led into several driveways.

The Prescotts' house was a three-story colonial with a two-car garage. It was set at the top of a small hill and surrounded by a semicircle of pines that seemed too perfectly placed to be natural. Half the lights in the house were on, and two lit rooms on the top floor seemed to stretch the green-and-white fence into a smiling jack-o'-lantern. A guy and a girl sat on the front steps puffing a joint, and I could hear the muffled sounds of a boom box. Otherwise, you wouldn't have been able to tell it was a party.

"Is that Jeremy Prescott?" I asked.

"Nah," Dave said. "That's the center for Dwiggins—eighteen points per."

When Jarvis and Danny arrived, we walked up the cobblestone path to the front door. My joints and muscles still ached from being chased, but I wasn't about to ask for an Advil. Adrenaline would have to do.

"Brits drive on the wrong fucking side of the road," Danny said, leaning toward me.

Evergreen bushes lined the sides of the walkway and, as we

reached the top, I saw a young guy lying smack in the middle of one of the shrubs. He was passed out and snoring violently.

"Any peeps show?" Dave asked the basketball player.

"Same derelicts," the girl said, nodding.

"Same dereliction," Dave added.

We walked through the coatroom and into the main living room. The walls were painted a stark white and decorated with a collection of African masks. They reminded me of pieces that my father used to collect, and I wanted to ask where they were from. A pool table sat along the far wall near two gigantic, light blue couches.

Three girls were lounging on the near couch, each with a tall glass of red wine, and the coffee table was layered with pasta dishes and slices of chocolate mousse cake. On the other couch, a young guy sat clutching a bottle of Stoli and sniffing remnants of coke. Two of the girls started laughing, and one of them spilled a slosh of wine on the couch. I think I was the only person who noticed.

"Who wants sushi?" one of the girls shouted, picking up the cordless.

"That Nippon place is whack," the guy muttered. "Sushi's mad dry by the time it gets here."

"Don't worry, darling." She smiled and pulled out her gold card. "My tekka maki will be here before you can say *Enola Gay*."

"That's Jeremy?" I asked Dave.

"Nah. That's one of our newest Dignitaries."

There are two types of parties. There's the raging, cop-calling, hard, blunted house party that seems to end itself, like

Sara's. Then there's the house party that doesn't ever really begin or end. People cluster and disperse. There are moments of ecstatic pleasure followed by boredom, but there's no panic. Instead, there's this sense that everyone is partying because they don't know how to stop anymore, or what that would even mean. I could still remember what it felt like—the stiffness, the fourth and fifth highs—I didn't miss it.

Dave motioned for Danny and me to follow him up a staircase. I was glad to get out of there. Each step was littered with dozens of CDs, like someone had spilled a Case Logic on the way down. I tried not to step on any of them but I couldn't help it.

On the second floor, Dave led us down a long hallway lined with bedrooms. As I passed each room, I caught half-second views of two or three or four kids lost in their own little worlds. In one bedroom, there were three hoods eating take-out Chinese food, taking glass bong hits, and playing Mario Cart on N64. The next room had two kids from Dwiggins and a pair of black lights. Nobody was moving, and nobody was planning on moving.

At the end of the hall, Dave showed us into a den with a bunch of guys. Each of them was dressed in a well-pressed designer suit, and their hairdos were meticulously gelled. Everyone else at the party looked like they were two hits away from passing out, and these guys were ready to shoot the back cover of *GQ*. What the hell was going on?

"Where's Greg?" I asked. "He was supposed to be here."

"Lust gots held up with some business," Dave said. "Don't worry. He'll be here in a few."

Danny and I fell into a black leather couch in the corner and

I studied the players. One of the guys was staring out the window, cleaning his nails with a mangled paper clip, and another was impatiently flipping the bezel of his teardrop cuff link, open-close, open-close. Eventually, two of the suits eyeballed Danny and me, and Dave gave them both a reassuring nod. I didn't recognize any of the guys, and they didn't seem to care about us. They were waiting for something else, and none of them looked patient.

A guy stood up from his armchair and ran his fingers along a seamless half-Windsor. "Gentlemen, in a moment."

Dave was sitting on the arm of our couch. I leaned toward him. "Jeremy?" I whispered.

He shook his head. "That's Kevin Joseph. Some philosophy freak who just dropped out of Princeton. He's mad proper, but he's good peoples."

"Why'd he drop out?" Danny asked.

"Boy had trouble leaving the city."

"So who are the rest of these guys?" I asked, wiping my palms on my jeans. I was ready to head for the door.

"They're all crazy high up in one crew or another. That's Zach Delsner of 3IC, that's Andrew Blank. Boyz don't look like hoods, huh? They kinda run shit without getting their hands dirty."

"Since when did hoods start wearing suits?" Danny asked.

"Oh, well, this shit's mad special," Dave declared.

The Princetonite was wearing a dark blue Armani suit that I'd seen in the *Times* magazine, and he was smoking a More menthol. He wiped his nose conspicuously. "Welcome to the fourth annual meeting," he said, picking up a remote control and pointing it at the VCR. A handheld image of a teenage girl standing outside a restaurant jumped onto the TV screen. She was wearing a dark cardigan, and she looked nervously back and forth along the avenue. Someone was filming her from the building across the street, and she obviously had no idea she was being taped. Kevin paused the video.

"I'd call the roll, but we all know each other." He reached down to the coffee table, pushed away a rolled-up hundred-dollar bill, and grabbed another cigarette.

"Again, I'm glad all of you could make it," Kevin began. He smiled and pointed at the television. "Gentlemen, we are all professionals in one of the rarest recreational sports out there. What we do isn't pretty."

Kevin gestured and enunciated like he was giving a carefully studied lecture to this small gathering. Two of his friends laughed and encouraged his building rhythm. I had no idea what the hell he was talking about. Part of me didn't even want to know. When the hell was Greg going to get here?

"It isn't pretty, and yet, it's beautiful. I know you've all invested a lot of time in this project, and we all have a good deal of money riding on it. Needless to say," Kevin said, pausing, "this is important."

Kevin hit "play." The girl was still standing on the sidewalk, looking completely lost. He pulled an envelope from his jacket pocket and read: "Jill Browning. Sophomore, five-foot-six, one hundred and nine pounds. Grew up on East 86th, then moved to 92nd and Fifth. Father, Richard, works at NYU Medical and mother, Judith, is a CPA turned homemaker. Jill did K through eighth at Spaulding, then enrolled at Groves in the fall. Her interests are pottery, E. M. Forster novels, world hunger, and Romance languages. Boyfriend status: none."

Danny looked over at Dave. "What is this?"

"Just enjoy it," Dave said, grinning. "Greg'll be here in a couple."

The video played on, and by now Jill was standing at a pay phone booth. I could tell by the frame on the shot that they were using a digital camera, and I could hear the lens banging against the windowsill.

"She's speed-dialing, yo," one of the guys shouted.

"She waited seven and a half minutes. Then she made two phone calls," Kevin said. "The second call was to Teddy's house."

"Who answered?"

"We had Jason there to answer the phone."

"Was she heated Teddy's ass was late?" the guy on the far couch asked. "Bitch looks crazy upset."

On the television, Jill walked back across the street to the restaurant. She had this anxious look on her face that made me feel even worse for her.

"She was nervous, but I wouldn't say Jill was upset," Kevin said. "Jason told her that Teddy's mother was yelling at him and that he was running late. It was all done with a good deal of tact."

An older-looking guy with slicked blond hair threw his arms in the air. "When we gonna start winning bills?"

I turned and saw Greg walk into the room. He was wearing a long black ski jacket and a Dodgers hat, and he laughed softly at the television. We made eye contact and Greg sat down between Danny and me.

"Wazzup, Thet?" Greg said. "Diggs to the rescue." We had a long handshake, both of us waiting for the other one to let go. Greg probably dreamed about this. "You Mr. Clean?" he asked, looking over at Danny.

Danny reached to shake Greg's hand. "She dragged me into the bathroom."

"Ten and a half minutes," the blond-haired guy shouted. "One of you herbs is out. Come on," he cried, scanning his friends. "I know somebody's out."

A guy who hadn't opened his mouth yet threw a roll of twenty-dollar bills onto the coffee table. It looked like about three or four hundred dollars, but the rubber band was wrapped so tightly I couldn't really tell. "Shit was a long shot," he muttered. "You fucked me, Kevin, with this Groves bittie. I wouldn't have taken these odds on some boarding-school piece. Bitch'll wait there all fucking night."

Danny leaned toward me. "They're betting on how long they can keep her on that corner. Right?"

Greg nodded. "We've got it down to this crazy science. Boyz bet using a yearbook photo and a bunch of other stats, but only the emcee knows her name in advance."

"How do you bet?" I asked.

"Like *The Price Is Right,* 'cept with minutes."

"Kevin doesn't remind me of Bob Barker," Danny said.

"Any other rules?" I asked.

"Nah. You can't call her celly if she got one. Shit's too easy that way. But she can call the guy."

"And the winner gets the pool?" Danny asked.

"For starters."

"What else?" Danny said, squinting at the television.

Greg smiled. "I wish I could tell you boyz, but it's club rules." I'd never even heard of anything like this before. The toughest prep-school hoods didn't feel guilt—they felt like gods.

Jill shook her head angrily and walked to the curb. She stared anxiously down the street, like she was about to hail a cab. The room exploded with laughter.

"She's out."

"Not a chance," Zach Delsner said under his breath.

"Bitch, get in the cab," Andrew groaned.

"Not a chance in hell," Zach repeated.

I needed to get out of there—I couldn't watch this. "What's the plan?" I said, trying to get Greg's attention.

"We're meeting them tomorrow at four. Everybody's gonna be there who needs to be."

"It's all cool?" I asked.

"Trust me," Greg said. "Four o'clock at Trinity Church on Morningside."

"A church?" Danny asked.

"Yeah, who's gonna throw down in a church?" Greg said, turning back to the television. "We'll round up at three-thirty, outside Max's Hot Dogs."

Zach pointed at the television. "My womans," he cried as Jill stepped off the curb and back underneath the awning. "That doe-eyed Betty will cook dinner streetside before walking out on Teddy."

"Twelve and a half minutes," the blond-haired guy shouted.

Andrew tossed his money onto the pile. He placed three small vials of coke on the coffee table and then searched for more. "Teddy's crazy good-looking," he exclaimed. "He needs to be a little busted. She's probably been sweating him for years."

Danny tapped Greg on the shoulder. "Why aren't you playing?"

"I was barred from this round," he said. "I recognized her from my Sunday school, and they consider that inside info. My boyz take it mad seriously." Greg stood up and fixed his jacket. "I'm gonna go catch the end of the Clips game. Feel free to crash here. Everything's gonna chill out once this shit's over."

"You're not gonna stay to see the end?" I asked, disgusted.

"It's crazy boring unless you got bills riding on it," Greg said, winking at me.

I used to think I understood Greg. I mean, underneath it all. Two weeks before eighth-grade midterms, I caught him crying in the fire staircase over some physics test he'd goose-egged. He never admitted it to me, but Greg had a million different learning disabilities, and I knew he was terrified of reading aloud in class or being called to the blackboard. All the stret cred used to mean that nobody would talk shit to Greg, but that was gone. Tonight, he was running on rage. I think I actually missed my old friend.

The blond-haired guy jumped to his feet and gestured wildly at the television. Another girl was standing on the street corner talking to Jill. "Who the fuck is that?"

"Some friend of hers," Kevin said. "It's random."

"That's interference, yo," Andrew shouted. "Shit's a let."

"Fuck you, let," Zach said in a monotone. "It's part of the playing field."

"Who's the bittie?"

Kevin shrugged. "I don't know. I showed the tape to another guy from Groves, but he didn't recognize her."

"That bitch is a plant," Andrew said, looking around the room anxiously. "This is mad fixed."

"It's grace." Zach beamed. "That piece's gonna buy me a new Rolex."

"Fuck your plant," Andrew said, sulking.

Zach laughed. "Hey, boyz, it's hard being God's favorite."

The blond-haired guy sank back into the couch. "Bitches always be bumping into each other."

I nudged Danny. "Let's get out of here."

Danny nodded and we both stood up.

The blond-haired guy tossed what had to be nearly a thousand dollars onto the coffee table. The wad of money made a solid *thud* when it landed, and everybody looked over at him. He shook his head. "I'm gonna cut that bittie."

———

Downstairs, the Dignitary who'd been partying with the girls was now snoring underneath the coffee table and two cats were picking at the leftovers. The girls were gone. The girls are always gone.

I opened a blue wooden door off the living room, and Danny and I walked into the kitchen. The center table was completely covered. There was a half-eaten cheesecake, two empty cans of chili, piles of clementine rinds, a dozen little bottles of Pellegrino, and the remains of a roll of Pillsbury cookie dough. On the counter were three twenty bags of weed, a couple joints, and two pitchers of mixed drinks.

I pulled out a chair and sat down. I needed a break. It was exhausting dealing with Greg and the Diggs and whoever else was upstairs. Maybe I was just out of practice.

Danny walked over to the refrigerator, grabbed a Heineken, and tossed it to me. Opening the two cupboards above the refrigerator, he found a bottle of Stoli and tossed the cap into the sink. He threw the bottle back and punished it.

"Don't you get tired of getting wasted?" I asked, looking down at the light green label of my beer. "It's not gonna fix anything."

"What else feels better?" Danny stepped over to the counter and picked up two joints. "They leave the skunkweed out," he said, flipping me one.

I tucked the joint behind my ear. "What about love?"

"Why?" Danny walked back over to the refrigerator. "So I can be like you?"

"Fuck you," I muttered. I was risking my ass for him, and he knew it.

"I didn't mean that personally. It's just that I don't buy it."

"You don't know what you're talking about," I said, but maybe he did.

"Hey, listen, I know I'm the bad guy in this movie."

"Your life isn't a movie," I said, more to myself than to him. "You're not that important."

"I am to me, Nick." He pulled out a container of fresh-squeezed orange juice and poured it into the bottle of Stoli. Danny placed his finger over the top of the bottle and gave it a couple good shakes.

I heard the kitchen door swing open, and I looked over my shoulder. Kris stood there with her long black hair tucked casually inside her collar. I felt like jumping up and running over to her, but I wasn't going to let her make an ass out of me again.

"Stage direction." Danny laughed. "Girl enters room."

Kris walked over to Danny and wrapped her arms around his shoulders. He sagged back into a chair.

"Kris, I'm so touched you came all the way out here for me," he said, still grinning.

"What the hell is going on?"

"You want the short, medium, or long version?" Danny asked.

"The first two," Kris said, looking over at me. I couldn't tell if she was angry with me or angry with this whole damn mess. I hoped she realized what I was doing for her brother.

"There are about thirty kids with trust funds and coke habits trying to pound me for hooking up with this girl."

"And the medium?"

"That was the medium."

"And why the hell are we in Riverdale?"

Danny pointed at me. "Ask your friend, the gangsta."

"What's he talking about?" Kris asked.

"Greg said he'd help us settle this. As a favor to his old friend, Thet," I said.

"Hence the new outfit." Kris shook her head. "Isn't it a little crazy to trust Greg?"

"Danny doesn't have much choice. Besides, some people are so crazy, they have to be good at something."

"Even if it's breaking people's noses?" Kris asked.

"Especially if it's breaking people's noses," Danny declared.

"I guess I should thank you," Kris said.

I shrugged, trying to pretend like it didn't matter to me. This wasn't just about Kris, but I felt like she owed me.

Danny smiled and took another long swig. "I'm sending him fucking chocolates."

"Nick, can I talk to Danny for a second? Before he passes out."

"Me," Danny mumbled. "I'm just getting my second wind."

"Sure, I'm gonna . . ." I paused and tried to think where I could go. "I'm gonna go sit out by the pool," I said, picking up my backpack.

Danny saluted as I pulled open the back door and stepped out into the Prescotts' yard. On the patio, there were a couple of chaise longues and a barbecue set that someone had obviously started using and then forgotten about. The pool cover had slipped off the frame, and as I got closer, I saw that someone had tossed an empty keg into the center of the pool. The cover probably broke on impact and the bobbing weight had slowly twisted the plastic sheet toward the bottom. It was so contorted that it must have been sinking for hours, and I couldn't decide whether it was starting to look like a light blue carnation or a whirlpool in slow motion.

I kicked a fleece blanket off a chaise and sat down. I slid the joint out from behind my ear. Pulling the first, hot drag, I felt the smoke spill down my throat and burn my nostrils. From outside, I could hear the sounds of the guys upstairs replaying Jill's wait on the corner, and through the living-room doors I could make out the Dignitary sleeping underneath the coffee table. I took two more hits and stamped the rest out. I didn't want to get stupid in front of Kris.

Kodak and I used to love to sneak away from a house party and find a quiet place to chill. We called it Book Clubbing, because we'd always borrow a book or two off the host's bookshelf, and Kodak would usually swipe a bottle of wine. Half the time we'd end up reading on the roof of a building or in a back stairwell, but it was always the perfect way to balance out a long night of partying. Kodak loved the irony of reading a novel in the middle of all of the debauchery and mayhem. We never talked much during Book Club, but I didn't mind. Kodak and I understood each other.

I unzipped my backpack and grabbed a can of Krylon. Giving it an even shake, I sprayed a streak into the grass and a thin film gathered on the top of my forefinger. The paint felt cool on my skin, and I rubbed my fingertips together. I brushed the Krylon off into the grass and remembered how the paint on my hands would always leave marks on my cigarette butts.

After a couple of minutes, Kris opened the back door and walked outside. Her lower lip was trembling like a five-year-old who'd scraped her knee, but she smiled when she saw me. Kris sat down at the foot of my chaise and let out a long sigh.

"I'm a wreck," Kris said. "I just spoke to my mom. They started throwing bottles at the front door again, and she called the cops. She's a fucking wreck, too."

My mouth was dry. "Did you tell her where we were?"

"I told her Danny was on his way to Jersey to stay with a friend. Danny needs to settle this."

"Where'd you say you were?"

"With Luke."

"Huh," I muttered. "Why didn't Luke come with you?"

"He might be playing in some gig later tonight."

I nodded. "Danny asleep?"

"Yeah, he found a guest bedroom downstairs. You know, I really owe you for this, Nick. I mean, you must've swallowed your pride asking Greg."

"Greg's loving every minute of this."

"I'm sure." Kris lay down next to me in the chaise. "How about you tell me a story?" she whispered. "I need to get out of my head, Cowboy."

I put my arm around Kris's shoulders and hugged her softly. She'd never let me get this close to her. It felt amazing. "What kind of story?"

"I don't know. You know any love stories?"

"I don't think so."

"Come on. I won't tell any of your guy friends. Promise." Kris rested her head on my chest and tucked her hands inside her sleeves. I leaned forward, grabbed the fleece blanket, and wrapped it around us. She grinned and closed her eyes. I couldn't say no.

"Okay, let me think. I guess it was the summer after seventh grade, and there was this girl, Michelle, at my tennis camp. Well, she had me completely strung out. Cupid must've been using a semiautomatic that day. And being the romantic seventh-grader I was, I got this idea into my head that I'd just sweep her off her feet."

"And into your arms."

"Right . . . Well, I taped a long-stemmed rose to the outside of her locker in the rec room." I could feel the rise and fall of

Kris's rib cage against my chest. At that moment, I would've done the entire weekend over again just to be lying there next to her. "God, I remember standing next to locker one-twelve with this enormous rose hidden under my jacket."

"A red rose?"

"A rose is a rose."

Kris looked inquisitively up at me.

"It was red," I conceded. "Anyway, my heart was pounding for the rest of the day. I was so scared to see her on the courts and have her realize it was me."

"Why would that have been so bad?"

"I don't know," I said. "Well, that night I wrote her this letter confessing everything and saying I thought she was brilliant and funny and drop-dead gorgeous. I slipped it into her locker the next day, but I didn't sign it."

"Why?"

"You'll see. So that afternoon I sit down next to her during a water break and say, 'Did I forget to sign my letter?'"

Kris burst out laughing and covered her face with her hands. "What'd she say?"

"We talked for a bit, and eventually she told me she had a crush on this guy in AA Singles."

"That sucks," Kris said, still smiling.

"She said I couldn't feel as strongly as my letter said I did. She gave me that 'You don't even know me' line."

"And then she went back to her forehand volleys."

"It really bothered me that she didn't . . ." I paused. "I just gave her my heart, and she didn't get it."

Kris nodded. "'Doubt thou the stars are fire; doubt that

the sun doth move; doubt truth to be a liar; but never doubt I love.'"

"What's that from?"

"Hamlet."

"Well, at least I'm not the only one who dies in the end."

"Oh, come on," Kris groaned. "What happened to that grade-school romantic?"

"I wish I knew."

"Don't get too cynical, Cowboy," Kris said, shaking her head gently. "I think what you did was great."

I pulled Kris closer to me. My pulse was speeding from the joint, and I thought about Danny lying passed out in bed and how furious Mrs. Prescott would be when she found the keg in her pool. A soft breeze swept Kris's hair across my neck, and I let my chin rest on her shoulder. She looked over at me and smiled. I caught her eyes as soon as I began to raise my head and held them. Her smile settled but I never let go of her eyes.

"Kris, I love you."

One . . .

Two . . .

"What?" Kris said, startled.

"I'm in love with you, Kris." I wanted to tell her everything.

"Oh, my God."

"I had to tell you."

"I . . ." She hesitated.

"Kris. I've been in love with you—"

"Wait," Kris interrupted.

"Ever since we met." I'd rehearsed it so many times in my head, every word and every phrase came rushing at me.

"Slow down."

"I could have sworn you knew."

"I didn't," she whispered.

"Does that make me clever or stupid?" I asked, searching her face. She didn't look ecstatic, but she didn't look unhappy either.

"Neither."

"Maybe you weren't looking." As soon as I said that, I regretted it. I'd given her an easy way to let me down.

"I don't know what to say."

"You don't have to say anything." I tried to sound reassuring, but my fingers were trembling.

"Nick," she began, and I froze. "Can you give me some time? I mean, with Danny and everything else. I'm going to need time to figure this all out."

"Fine," I said. "As much as you need."

"I just know that I'm glad you told me. I mean, you could've tried something or whatever, but you did the right thing."

"Okay," I said. "But Kris, can you promise me something?"

"Sure."

"Michelle doubted me. Promise me you won't."

"I promise." Kris nodded, and the few locks of her hair resting on my shoulder nodded too. "I don't doubt you." She paused for a second. "I think I need to go for a walk," she said, sitting up. "Maybe do some writing."

"You'll need to steal a pad of paper."

"I'm always prepared, Cowboy." She pulled a tiny notebook out of her jeans pocket. "Can you get some sleep?"

Kris vanished before I could think of anything else to say. I guess I didn't have anything left to say. Resting my head back against the chaise, I slipped Ella out of my wallet. I rolled him back and forth between my fingers, like a poker player in those old Westerns. If my dad were around, he could tell me what to do next.

I knew one thing, though. This was the last time I'd ever have to fall asleep not knowing what would happen if I told Kris. I slid the coin back into my pocket and closed my eyes.

———

The first thing I felt were Kris's lips pressing against mine. Without opening my eyes, I reached for her and ran my hand slowly across her cheek. Her kisses nipped at my chin, then slid their way down my neck. I pulled her toward me and her lips fell back onto mine. Kris's soft breathing tickled my nose, and all I could think was *She really loves me.*

"That's my answer," she whispered.

"I can live with this," I said, opening my eyes.

"I was wondering when you were going to open them."

"I was scared it was a dream. I didn't want to chance it." Kris's eyes were teary and beginning to swell. "What happened?"

"I was just crying a little," she said, wiping her nose.

"No, I can see you were crying. I mean what happened?" I suddenly had so much energy I didn't know what to do with myself. I felt like running around the Prescotts' yard, but I didn't want to let go of Kris.

"I don't know." She climbed into my arms and rested her head on my chest. "Can we go inside? It's freezing out here."

"I'm sure we can find a place to crash."

We walked back through the living room. Only the cats were still around. Upstairs, a guy from Troy was lying stretched out on the sofa in the study, and he had a bag of mushrooms sitting on the coffee table next to a bottle of Evian. He was desperately clutching a remote control in his left hand, playing with the volume levels on C-SPAN2 reruns.

Kris and I found an empty bedroom next door. It was a small room with a couple pizza cartons, but it would have to do. Kris walked over and hit the light switch. The overhead bulb flickered for a few seconds, then flooded the room with green light. Someone had taken the light fixture off and replaced the original bulb with a cheap fluorescent one.

Kris looked up at the ceiling and shook her head. "Give me a break," she groaned.

Sitting on the bed, I turned on the table lamp.

Kris flipped off the overhead and leaned against the flowered wallpaper. "You know, I once heard a rumor about you."

"From who?" I slid my hand into my jeans pocket and pulled out my pack of cigarettes.

"It was a while ago," Kris said. "I think we'd just started hanging out."

"What'd you hear?" I asked, nervously blowing the smoke up toward the ceiling.

"That you hooked up with all these girls from some high-school hockey team," Kris said, grinning. "Somewhere in Canada or something."

"What?" I had no idea why she was bringing this up.

"That's just what I heard," Kris declared.

I walked over to her and placed my hand on her hip. I needed to kiss her again.

Kris looked down at my hand. "Well, is it true?"

"No. It was a rumor sophomore year."

She smiled. "None of it's true?" She coolly brushed my hand off and walked over to the window. She'd never flirted with me like this before. I loved it.

"There was a girl. She was from Canada. And I slept with her in the Bahamas."

"What about the rest of them?" Kris asked, pulling open the shades.

"That's the fiction. She was my first, and one of my friends leaked the gossip. One thing led to another, and the Canadian girl became a hockey team."

"Does that include the goalie?" She sat down on the windowsill.

"Depends on the version," I said, leaning up against the window frame.

"Why didn't you stop it?"

"I tried, but it was too late. Besides, Tim thought it was the greatest piece of gossip he'd ever heard. After a while, I think he started making shit up just to keep it going. You know Tim."

"It didn't sound like you anyway," Kris said, running her hand along my leg. My calf started to shiver and I pressed my foot firmly into the carpet.

Through the wall came a piercing Southern accent. "And the distinguished gentleman from North Carolina has made several important claims in regard to . . ."

"Turn it down," I yelled.

". . . and for the direct aid of the various congressional organizations . . ." The volume dropped off and was followed by a muddled apology.

"Why'd you wait to ask me about it?" I said, trying to regain Kris's attention.

"It never mattered that much to me until . . ." Her voice faded out.

"Until?"

"Until it did. . . ." She reached under my shirt and pressed her fingers against the small of my back. She must've felt my goosebumps. "So what's the real story?" Kris stood up before I could lean over to kiss her and walked to the bed. She sat down on the edge of the quilt, propped a pillow against the headboard, and lay back.

"Why are you so interested?" I asked, embarrassed.

"Come on," she said. "If everybody in your grade knew . . ."

I stepped toward her and ran my hand through her hair. I didn't want to think about anything else but Kris. "I was fifteen. Her name was Jenna. We were really drunk," I said. "That's it."

"Was it that fast?" she asked, looking up at me playfully.

"Shut up," I said, grinning.

"Fine, you do the talking."

"I was on vacation." I sat down next to her on the mattress.

"With your family?"

"Yeah. Are you sure you really want to hear this?"

"I wouldn't have asked."

"Okay." I shrugged. "So this kid and I were hanging out at the Holiday Inn on the beach. There was some bar outside with a calypso band."

"Red, red wine," Kris sang, laughing.

"Very funny." I sat back on my elbows. "Well, we're sitting

outside, and this girl at the table next to us keeps making eye contact with me. She wasn't amazing-looking, but she had this nice chin-length brown hair." I pushed my shoes off and let them fall to the floor. "I mean, I'd love to say that my first time was with this Marilyn Monroe who thought that I was God's gift to women, but . . ."

"I'd know you were lying."

"Right. So, I'm playing it cool, just seeing what'll happen, and she walks over to me."

"Just like that?" Kris asked.

"Pretty much." I leaned forward and pulled on Kris's shoelace. The knot didn't give and I ended up jerking her ankle. Fuck.

Kris pushed the shoe off with her other foot. "This isn't one of those girls who plays hard to get."

"Well, we got along really well. I mean, I'd spoken to a half dozen girls that night, and she was the first one who could've told me who won the Civil War."

Kris slid off her other shoe. "What'd you talk about?"

"Music, movies, where we lived." I lay down next to Kris and kissed her softly on the neck. "So we hung out together for a few hours, drinking these strawberry daiquiris, dancing a little, smoking all my cigarettes. You know the bit. God, I think we even walked down to the beach and named the stars."

"How romantic," Kris said. "And then?"

I smiled and shook my head. I couldn't believe I was telling her this story. "So out of nowhere she has this sudden urge to go swimming. Well, we were in that beginning stage where everything seems like foreplay so I said sure. And right out there in the middle of the ocean, we started screwing around."

"I'm surprised you didn't drown," Kris said, tugging gently at my hair.

"No kidding. I swallowed about a quart of salt water trying to doggie paddle and kiss at the same time."

"Sounds good, if you can get past the salty taste."

"When we got back to the beach we just kept going at it. And within like five minutes we were rolling around in the sand." I lifted Kris's sweater over her head and her hair scattered across her breasts.

"Were you nervous?" Kris asked, pulling my hoodie over my shoulders.

"Hell, I was as nervous as the kid picked last for dodgeball."

Sliding my left hand down Kris's back, I tripped on her bra strap and felt for plastic. I ran my hand across the belt of fabric—I couldn't find the clasp. Giving up for the moment, I went back to kissing Kris's neck. She took my hand in hers, placed my fingers delicately in between her breasts, and guided me to the clasp. I tensed the elastic strap and unhooked her bra.

"So what happened?" Kris asked, skimming her fingers along my belt.

"Isn't it the same for everyone? I mean, more or less." I kept trying to hold on to my composure. I'd spent so many hours wondering what her breasts actually looked like and then they were wonderful.

"I hope it wasn't less," Kris whispered. "How come you never told me that story before?" she said, smiling.

"You've gotta be kidding me." I leaned over and flicked off the lamp.

———

Kris lay across me on the bed. Her arm was wrapped securely around my waist, and her head was tucked in the hollow of my neck, like she was checking to see if I was still breathing. I couldn't believe it—I'd done it. I felt like going around and thanking all the furniture in the bedroom. I didn't understand how things had come together so perfectly, but I was ready to fall to my knees and praise anything that had played a part.

Kris slid two fingers down the middle of my rib cage and scratched at my belly button. I let my hand slope down her back and pressed my thumb into her soft skin. I felt like I was holding her with just my fingertips.

"How you doing?" I whispered.

"Good," Kris sighed.

I kissed her collarbone. "Me too."

"I just wish I wasn't so worried about my brother."

I didn't know what to say. I'd forgotten about everything else that was going on outside our guest bedroom, but I guess I couldn't blame her for worrying.

"He gets so cocky and sarcastic," she said. "But he's not tough, you know."

"I know. He's book tough," I said, searching for a smile.

"He's really fragile," she mumbled.

"We're doing everything we can."

Kris and I lay there in silence and listened to the ceiling fan drift. The house was sleeping, but I could hear the trees wrestling outside our window. I looked over at my hoodie and studied the tiny red specks on the arms. I couldn't tell if it was blood or paint.

"What are you thinking about?" Kris asked.

"Greg . . . and Kodak," I said, reaching for my pack of Luckies on the nightstand. I ran a match down the wall behind us, and it threw light onto the faded wallpaper. Kris closed her eyes, and the burning sulfur drew the shadows from her eyelashes down her cheeks.

"What about them?"

"I just tried to bury it all. I mean, everything around me said to forget about them and the art. And poof, I was Nick again."

"They're called adolescent phases. Everybody has them."

"But I didn't quit." I placed the cigarette between my lips. "I mean, it's not like I suddenly got sick of the phase."

"Of course not," Kris said, reaching for a drag. "One of your best friends was nearly killed."

"It was more than that."

"How do you mean?"

"It's hard to explain."

"Try me." Kris rubbed her chin against my chest.

I wanted to tell Kris but I wasn't sure that I could. I'd spent so many hours talking to myself about that night—I couldn't make sense of it anymore. Kris always had a way of clarifying things and, lying there next to her, I trusted her with her everything I had. I opened my mouth but no words came out. Take two. "Kris?"

"Yeah."

"If I tell you something, can you promise me you'll never repeat it?"

"Sure, Cowboy. You always know that."

"No, this is different," I said, trying to steady my voice. "This is something I've never told anyone. I mean, I don't even think I've ever spoken the words or whatever."

"What is it?" Kris said, looking up at me.

———

Greg rolled onto his back and tried to push himself up off the pavement. Kids were yelling at him to stand up. A hood lifted Kodak by the belt and launched him into a car door. I couldn't move. Why couldn't I move? I would've given anything for one of the hoods to punch me or knock me down, to drag me into the fight, but nobody even noticed I was there.

Six hoods circled Kodak and each one of them took turns attacking him, like wolves. I saw the flash of a butterfly knife swinging open, and then Kodak wilted onto the pavement. I thought I was going to throw up. I needed to scream but my whole body was shaking. Greg scrambled to his feet and threw an empty punch into one of the hoods; the guy laughed. And then, without saying a word, the hoods jumped the park wall and faded into Central Park.

I ran over to Kodak and fell to my knees. Lifting his head in my hands, I felt his staggered breathing. "Oh, fucking shit," I cried. "Somebody call an ambulance."

Kodak's hands were gripping his side and his feet shuffled slowly back and forth against the pavement. His eyes were pressed closed but I could see his tears blending into the sweat on his cheeks. There was blood, so much blood.

"I'm so sorry, Charlie. I'm so fucking sorry."

Greg used a fender to lift himself up. The crowd of kids scattered into a million pieces; only the cab driver remained. How could they leave us like this?

"Get a fucking ambulance," Greg shouted, clutching his jaw.

Kodak's left eye slid open and he stared up at me. "Did they get you, Nick?"

Sirens ricocheted down the avenue. Greg was hunched over, vomiting.

"I'm okay," I whispered. I was such a fucking coward. "The ambulance is nearly here, Charlie. Nearly here, okay?"

Kodak nodded and squeezed his side. His other hand reached for my arm and left bloody fingerprints across my hoodie. "I can't believe they fucking stabbed me."

I grabbed Kodak's hand and hugged it against my chest. "Stay quiet, man. Okay?"

"I'm fucking freaked-out, Nick."

"I know," I said. "Me, too."

———

Kris lifted her cheek from my chest. "You can trust me."

"The night Kodak was stabbed . . . I mean the fight . . . I just stood there."

Kris looked at me with a troubled expression on her face, and I shut my eyes. Darkness. Suddenly, I wanted to yell at her for listening, but I couldn't do anything until my breathing started again.

"Nick? Are you okay?"

Cold air splashed down my throat. "I just stood there," I said, surprised by the sound of my own voice. "I watched. It must've been like two minutes."

"I don't understand," Kris whispered. "What—"

"I could've helped him, and I didn't do a fucking thing, didn't move."

"I get it." She nodded.

"I've never told anyone, you know," I said. "Not Greg or Tim or anybody. I just stood there and watched my best friend die."

Kris massaged my shoulders. "But he didn't die, Nick."

"Part of him did."

Kodak never snapped back. He was out of the hospital in ten weeks, and his body fully recovered, but he wasn't the same guy; he wasn't even close. The doctors said the bleeding had flooded his lungs and they weren't able to determine how long he'd gone without air. Instead of being his talkative, nervous self, Kodak became this really sweet, gullible kid. Almost childlike. Part of him just evaporated that night, and I hadn't done a damn thing to try and stop it.

After Kodak got home from the hospital, his parents decided to move the family to Dallas. Between Kodak's sister and Kodak, they'd had enough of New York. I understood why but I hated them for taking him away. His parents found some special boarding school in Fort Worth, for kids with disabilities or whatever, and Kodak actually seemed excited to go.

"Do you ever write him or call?" Kris asked. "I mean, since you think about him so much."

I rubbed at my throat. "I sent him two letters. Nothing back."

I'd visited Kodak at home a couple of times before he left. It was hell. The way his father would stare at me when he answered their front door, blaming me. The way his mother would check in on us every fifteen minutes. I tried to talk to Kodak about piecing and Greg, but all he ever wanted to discuss was classical music. I couldn't tell if he didn't remember or didn't want to remember or was ignoring me altogether. I just wanted my friend back.

"You could call," Kris said.

"I guess. He was in the city last weekend, and he didn't call me."

"He doesn't blame you."

"He should," I muttered.

"I'm so sorry, Nick."

"I am, too." I pulled the quilt over us and watched the shadows of branches and leaves paint circles on the far wall. I missed not having a movie playing in the background, drowning out my senses.

"Why didn't you jump in or . . . ?" Kris's voice faded.

"I don't know," I began. "I mean, I've never been a fighter. Like I've horsed around and shit, but never for real."

Kris kissed my forehead. "There's nothing wrong with that, Nick."

"I know," I sighed. "But there's something wrong with abandoning your friends. I mean, when they need you."

"Even though you would've ended up next to him in the hospital?"

"You don't know that," I said, trying to settle my stomach. "Trust me. If I knew what would've happened, I wouldn't . . ."

"What?"

"I'll just never know."

Kris leaned toward me. "It's okay to be afraid."

Why did she have to use that word? Is that what she thought? Is that what I thought? "It doesn't feel okay," I said.

"Besides, I don't even know if I was afraid. Sometimes, I think I was just too high or too drunk or too confused." I stared up at the moldings in the ceiling. "My father was never afraid."

Kris gently squeezed my hand. "I can't believe that," she said after a pause. "I mean, about your father."

"It feels that way."

"You know he wasn't as perfect as you remember him. I mean, he just couldn't have been."

If it had been anyone else saying that, I think I would've been furious. "You never even knew him," I said calmly.

"But I know you, Nick."

"And?"

"And I think you make everything harder on yourself. I've never heard you say something negative about your dad."

I knew she was right, but it didn't change the way I felt, the way I imagined him.

"He was a drunk," I whispered. I couldn't believe I'd said it—I couldn't believe it didn't feel bad to say. If I was laying my cards on the table, so was he. "And a cheat. But I still love him more than anybody else in the world." I didn't want Kris to see me cry. I'd promised myself a long time ago that I'd only cry on my own.

"Wow," Kris said, kissing my chest. "That wasn't easy to say."

I was exhausted. "I don't know why, but I feel like you deserve to know. I don't think he'd mind that I told you."

"Is that why your mother never talks about him?"

"Yeah." I nodded. "She threw away everything of his when we moved. She even wanted me to chuck Elvis, so I stuffed him in my wallet." Kris could never remember the name Ella-Asbeha, so she just called him The King or Elvis for short.

"It's incredible how you're never angry with him. I mean, you don't blame him for anything."

"Because I know he loved me more than anybody else ever will." I held my breath and waited for the hurt to pass. It spread across my chest and dissolved into my arms and fingers. I'd repeated those words to myself so many times before, but never out loud. "You know what I mean?"

Kris nodded slowly. "That's amazing."

"I guess." I let my cheek rest on hers. "It's just the truth."

"I know it is." She rubbed my stomach. "Do you ever dream about him?"

"I used to a lot. But now it's only like once a month. I still love hanging out with him in my head, though."

"That's nice," Kris said, tucking her body against mine.

Sunday

A car alarm woke me. I opened my eyes and rolled over. Kris was sitting in a chair with her bare feet resting on the edge of the windowsill. She'd put on yesterday's sweater and jeans, and she was using her thigh to balance her notebook.

"'Morning," I said, squinting at the sunlight. It was amazing, waking up and looking at Kris.

"'Morning."

I fixed my pillow. "How long have you been up?"

"A bit."

"What time is it?"

Kris shrugged.

"Do you feel like coming back to bed?" I asked, stretching.

"I'm good," she said, staring down at her notebook. Kris's voice was different. It was flat, almost hollow. "Thanks, though." There was no question about it.

"You sure?"

"Yup."

"Is anything up?"

"Nope." Kris looked over at me to see if she'd answered my question. "Just writing a little."

I sat up and scanned the room for my pants. My breath was horrible and my toothbrush was in another borough. "I'm gonna walk to a bodega and get some coffee. You want to take a walk?"

"No, I'm fine. I got some earlier," Kris said, pointing to a paper cup on the windowsill.

"You were up?" I suddenly felt like climbing underneath the quilt and sleeping the rest of the day away. What could've changed in a handful of hours?

"Yeah. I had a lot of trouble sleeping."

"You could've woken me."

"No need. I wanted to do some writing anyway. There are a lot of places two blocks that way," she said, gesturing behind her.

I picked my pants up off the floor. I wanted to start the morning all over again, but a cup of coffee would have to do. "I'll check'm out," I said, reaching for my hoodie. "Is Danny still asleep?"

Kris nodded and kept writing.

My toes smacked against something hard in my Timberland.

Pain shot up my leg. I yanked my boot off and shoved my hand inside. I could feel dull metal edges and I pulled out two brass knuckles. Greg must've dropped them in there during the night. I hated the idea that he'd seen us lying in bed together. Before Kris noticed what was going on, I slipped the knuckles into my jeans. It couldn't hurt to hold on to them, even if the asshole was just trying to freak me out.

Opening the door halfway, I looked back at Kris. "I'll be back in ten." I blew her a kiss, but she didn't look up.

Downstairs, I could smell someone cooking breakfast. I slid the kitchen door open a crack and peered in. The room was pitch-black. All the overheads were off, the shades were drawn, and the only light was coming from a burner on the stove. Two hoods stood over a frying pan wearing night-vision goggles. They were debating where they should sprinkle the weed in their cheddar omelets. I didn't feel like weighing in on the issue, so I let the kitchen door slip closed.

Outside, there was a trail of beer cans and butts leading up to the Prescotts' front door. A pair of Rollerblades was dangling from the neck of a basketball hoop and someone had left a couple of street hockey sticks lying out. I pushed my sleeves up to my elbows and started walking.

A few blocks from the house, I noticed a kid sitting against the side of the road reading a torn-up comic book. His wife-beater T was ripped and his charcoal pants looked like they were connected to a suit jacket he'd lost somewhere during the night. I remembered meeting him with some kids in a club near Hudson, but that was all. He started to stand up as I walked by, and I could see dark circles surrounding his eyes.

"Yo, excuse me," he began. "Can I bum a cig?"

"No problem," I said, sliding one out. He pulled out a thin lighter with a black leather body. "You gonna be okay?"

"Yeah," he muttered, and sat back down. "Shit's mad fierce, but it's gotta wear off sometime." He laughed a little and took a long drag. "Don't fuck with horse tranquilizers."

"I'll remember that." I couldn't wait to get upstairs and crawl back into bed with Kris. We needed a second take. Maybe she just wanted some time to herself.

"Hey," he said, "which way is Fieldston Road at?"

"Two blocks that way." I extended my hand for a shake. "I'm Nick. I think we've met before."

"Jeremy," he mumbled.

"Jeremy Prescott?"

"Oh," he said, smiling. "You must be one of my guests."

———

When I opened the door to our room, Kris was sitting on the bed writing. I placed my cup of coffee on the bedside table, fell onto the mattress beside her, and kicked off my shoes. Putting my arms around her waist, I lay down next to her. I loved being able to touch her.

Kris lifted my hand. "I need to take a shower," she said, standing up quickly.

"Fine." I didn't care what she did. I just wanted her to stop acting the way she was acting. What had I done wrong?

I found a loose strand in the quilt and started picking at it. "What were you writing?"

"Just stuff." She flicked on the lights in the bathroom and then leaned up against the door frame.

"Huh," I muttered. "I'm writing a story for school." I wanted to keep her talking. "Mr. Michaels told us we could write a short story instead of a paper."

"What's it about?" She wrapped her long, black hair around the back of her neck and then let it fall onto her pale shoulders. She looked so beautiful, but her face was tense, like she was waiting for somebody else to show up.

"It's about this guy and girl," I began.

"Who go to a house party," Kris continued, smiling.

"They find the body of a deer in the woods." For a second, I could've sworn she was back, but then her smile faded.

"Who killed the deer?"

"Their cousin."

"And what happens?" Kris said.

"That's where I run into trouble. I want them to bury the deer, but I can't explain why they would."

"So why should they?"

"I like the idea," I said jokingly.

"So write both," Kris declared.

"Which two?"

"The version you want to have happen and the one you think actually would. You'll know which is better."

"And what happens if that doesn't work?" I asked.

"Scrap it. Move on."

I felt like asking her what she'd done with my Kris, but I didn't even want to hear the answer. It couldn't have all been in my head. At least not last night.

"I'll be out in five minutes," Kris said, walking into the bathroom and shutting the door.

As soon as I heard Kris turn the shower on, I picked up the phone on the bedside table and called Tim.

"Tim," I whispered, reaching for my cup of coffee. "I'm freaking out."

"Where are you?"

"Jeremy Prescott's house in Riverdale."

"What?"

"I came here to meet up with Greg."

"Well, you should know Elliot's on the hunt for you. He's called me twice already."

"I don't have time to deal with that guy. He's useless." If I called Elliot, he'd cut me off immediately. All the asshole would care about is getting me home and grounding me. He just didn't give a shit. If my mother was really trying to make life without my dad easier for me, she shouldn't have married a traffic cop.

"Well, I told him you probably stayed at a friend's place."

"Tim," I began again, "Kris and I slept together last night."

"Wow," Tim shouted. "What happened?"

"I'm losing my shit."

"What do you mean?"

"Just listen to me for a second," I said, lying back against the mattress. "This morning, it's like she doesn't even want to be around me. I know Kris. Something's happened."

"Fuck."

"I don't want to lose her."

"I know, man," Tim said. "What do you think it could be?"

"I have no fucking clue. I mean, we talked after, and everything was great. And then I woke up, and she was writing, and she was just . . . different."

"How do you mean?" Tim asked.

"The way she was acting, talking. Everything."

"Nick, if I were you, I'd calm down and just see what happens. All this could be in your head."

"I guess."

The shower went off in the bathroom, and I heard the glass door sliding across the metal track.

"Just play it cool. That's what I'd do."

I took a deep breath. "I gotta go."

Kris opened the bathroom door and walked out in her jeans and sweater. Her hair was wrapped in a towel that she was balancing with her hand. "Can you get one of my hair thingamajigs?" Kris asked. "There's one on the table."

I couldn't take this. Either Kris loved me or she didn't. Either she wanted to be with me or she didn't. "Kris, can I ask you a question?"

"Sure."

I tossed her the scrunchee. "Was it a mistake?"

Kris paused like she'd misheard me. "What?"

"Us. Last night. I told you how I felt. I told you, and I didn't hold anything back."

"That was your choice," Kris said.

"So?"

"So there's no simple answer to a question like that. I mean, I've got so much going on right now, and Danny, and I'm just really . . ."

"There's an answer to every question," I said, annoyed. "I mean, outside, when you kissed me, all you said was 'I don't know.' What does that mean?"

"Just what it says."

"Kris, I love you. I told you that. But I have no fucking clue what's going on."

"I'm not trying to mess with your head," Kris said. "We spent the night together. Why can't we just leave it at that? There's no yes-or-no answer to these things."

I walked over to the window and looked down at the yard. The two guys from the kitchen were fencing with blue Styrofoam tubes that they must've found in the pool shed.

"You don't get it," I said.

"Then explain it to me."

"You know how when you like a guy, you think about him a lot. You imagine what it would be like for you to be together, your first kiss, hanging out, all that romantic stuff."

"Yeah."

"And when you kiss, and that part of your fantasy comes true, you don't know how much else will, too. I mean, you don't know whether he kissed you because he felt sorry for you or because he loves you."

Kris nodded. "If I kiss a guy, it means something."

"So when we kissed last night, I expected other things to be true, too."

"Like what?"

"I'm not sure," I said, lying. "All I know is that a kiss isn't just a kiss. Not between us, at least."

She sat down on the edge of the bed. "Nick, what do you want?"

"I need to know whether we just slept together and that was that, and it'll never happen again, or what. I mean, do you want me as a boyfriend, or is this just a one-night fling? I need to know, 'cause right now I feel like I don't know a thing."

There was a knock on the door. Kris looked at me as if she was about to say something, and then walked over to open it.

Danny stepped lazily into the room. The color was gone from his face, and I could see the beginnings of a mustache forming on his upper lip. He looked miserable. "Hey, Nick. I've got a riddle for you. What's the difference between tragedy and irony?"

"I don't know," I said.

"Self-importance." Danny walked into the bathroom and vomited three times, each one steadily lowering him to the tile floor. When he was finished, Danny was lying on the floor clutching the toilet bowl like a life preserver.

Kris walked over to him, knelt down, and rested her hand on his shoulder. "You're going to be okay," she whispered.

I could hear air brakes wheeze down the street as garbage men stopped to feed their trucks. My hands were so cold.

———

We called Ted's Taxis and a car pulled into the Prescotts' driveway fifteen minutes later. Kris spent the entire ride with her hair in front of her face like a veil and her hands clasped together, and I sat staring out the window, sneaking occasional glances at her profile. Danny was slumped between us, his head resting on my shoulder. I felt like such a fool. Things weren't supposed to happen this way.

When the taxi pulled up on Broadway, I grabbed my backpack and helped Danny out. The 242nd Street elevated station had two train tracks, and both were empty.

"How long till the next train leaves?" I asked the station attendant.

"Should be about fifteen minutes," she answered. "It's Sunday."

"Well, I'm gonna go get something to settle the stomach," Danny said, walking back toward the staircase. "You guys want anything?"

"Be back in ten minutes," Kris said firmly, and then he was gone.

I stared up at the clouds settling over Van Cortlandt Park. "The train ride shouldn't take that long." I couldn't look Kris in the eyes. I felt like as soon as I did, it would all be over.

"Yeah," she said.

Why was this happening? I'd told her everything last night. I'd told her things I didn't even know I could say.

Kris looked up at the sky. "What are you looking at, Cowboy?"

I wished she hadn't called me that. When she used that name, I thought of the first time we met and every day after. "Clouds," I said.

"I'm sorry we didn't get to finish our conversation."

"Kris, I said all I could say."

She shook her head slowly. "I don't love you, Nick. At least, not the way you want me to. But I think you already know that."

I bowed my head, and Kris continued talking. My eyes hurt. They stung.

"I liked being with you, but I'm not in love with you."

"Then why last night? Why the kiss?" I could feel a numbness spreading through my stomach.

"Because I wanted to give us a chance. For you and for me."

"That's the only reason?"

"And I guess there was part of me that wasn't sure," Kris said. "I wanted to be sure."

"I just don't get it."

"It's hard to explain. I sat up all morning writing about you, and me, and us. About relationships and Luke and—"

"Try," I interrupted. I could still smell her shampoo on my skin. Why did I have to sleep so well next to her?

Kris took a long, full breath. "You know how people say that they can't explain what love feels like. They always try and try, but it's impossible. Well, not being in love with somebody is just as difficult. I don't know why."

"Don't you ever think about it? I mean us."

"Sure, I've thought about it. I don't know." Kris paused. "Nick, I'm not your dream girl."

"How do you know?" I wanted to stare her down so she'd know what she was doing to me.

"Because the dream girl says yes," Kris declared. "She doesn't say no. I mean, that's part of being the dream girl. Natalie Wood didn't tell James Dean, 'Thanks, but no thanks.'"

"Do you miss Luke?" I asked. "I mean, do you still love him?"

Kris sighed. "Sometimes I think so. He wants me to go with him this summer, and I guess part of me really wants to. My father said we could stay with him for a while. I just don't know. . . ."

"If he's such a great guy, then why didn't he come with you last night?"

"That doesn't have anything to do with you and me," Kris said. "Nick, I'm sorry. I really am."

"I've got to go." I didn't have any idea where, but I felt like I had to leave. How could I stay?

I turned my back on Kris, and the Number 1 train that was pulling into the station, and walked as steadily as I could down the steps toward Broadway.

——

My legs felt as heavy as Wurlitzers when I stepped back onto the sidewalk. I was a disaster. This whole fucking weekend was a disaster. I walked underneath a white-and-green sign for Manhattan College and passed Doyle's Pub. On 239th Street, I walked by an empty parking lot with a young attendant asleep inside and a fruit stand with a spray-painted sign reading FRESH STRAWBERRIES. I couldn't understand how people were strolling by me so calmly.

I was just glad to be away from Kris. Half of me kept saying that it wasn't true, that she was sitting on the train realizing what a mistake she'd made, that she was about to pull the emergency cord—the other half of me was furious. How could she lead me on like that? I couldn't believe it, but Kris was more confused than I was. At least I knew what I wanted, even if I'd never have it.

On 238th, I walked past Vincent's pizza shop and stopped at the Five Star Restaurant. My mouth was so dry. I needed a soda. The grill man had his shirt half unbuttoned, and everybody at the counter looked like a regular. Sitting down on the first stool, I tried to get the waiter's attention. He was busy adjusting the top-shelf pies, and I gave up for the moment.

I didn't know what the hell to do with myself. When the girl of your dreams is your best friend, there's no one to talk to if things don't work out. Part of me wanted to scream at Kris for not seeing how amazing we could be together. Part of me just wanted to cry on her shoulder.

In the booth across from me, there was a little girl wearing a green cotton dress and a pair of white leggings, stretching down to white leather shoes. She was sitting on the edge of the cushion crayoning fiercely, but her legs barely reached the floor. There was a leather coat on the opposite seat and I decided that her father must be in the bathroom. Every few seconds she'd drop one crayon and snatch up another.

I must have looked like a total derelict, but I really felt like talking to somebody. I was lonelier now than I knew I could be.

"What are you drawing?" I said. "If you don't mind me asking."

She kept her eyes fixed on the paper, but her crayoning slowed. "A picture for my friend."

"What's it of?"

"Fishes," she said, slurring the last s.

"What kind?"

"Kissing fishes," she mumbled.

"Did you think them all up yourself?" I asked, trying to be friendly.

"I've got two at home," she said, looking up at me like I was dumb. "One's big and one's kinda small." She held up her drawing of a giant pink fish.

"Why are they called kissing fish?"

The waiter wandered down to my end of the counter, and I ordered a Coke.

"'Cause they have funny mouths when they swim," she said, stretching her mouth like a fish. "They look like they're kissing."

"Kissing what?"

"Kissing everything. The water, the plants, the rocks. Everything except each other."

I took a sip and chewed on a piece of ice. "They can't kiss each other?"

"Well, it kinda looks like they're kissing when they get all close, but they're not."

"What are they doing then?"

"Fighting," she said, picking up another crayon. "But it's not fair 'cause one's a lot bigger."

I nodded. "You're a good artist." Somebody deserved to feel good about themselves.

"Thank you." She smiled and reached for her fork.

I finished my soda and said good-bye to the girl. Walking back out onto Broadway, I tried to clear my head. I couldn't go back to the Prescotts and the Diggs, and there was no way I was going home. After losing Kris, it didn't really matter where I went.

I knew Greg would love it when I didn't show at the church. In his mind, it would prove all the shit he's ever said about me. He'd tell everybody about this, and the funny thing is that I didn't even care. None of that shit mattered to me.

Across the street, two Dalmatians were straining their necks against their leashes while they waited for the light to change. Their owner leaned back and tightened the hold. I lit a cigarette and tried to figure out which way to walk.

Kris and Danny were probably near 125th Street. I didn't

owe her a damn thing anymore. She'd made a fool of me for too long. I took another drag and tried to finish my thought.

Suddenly I saw Kodak's feet shuffling back and forth against the pavement and I could feel my legs sticking to the concrete. A car horn exploded in my ears—I was standing in the middle of the street. A middle-aged guy stuck his head out the window of an Acura and flipped me off. I couldn't move.

The horn sounded again. I leapt for the sidewalk. The Acura swerved angrily around the corner and I searched my pocket for Ella. He was mixed in with some change, but I recognized the texture of his face. Pulling him out, I squeezed him in my palm.

"What the fuck do I do now, Ella?" I whispered.

I remembered the way Danny had laughed when he tripped over the garbage cans Friday night, and how passionately he'd explained Conformism, and I realized this wasn't about Kris or Greg or Kodak anymore. I'd promised to help Danny—he needed me. I had to be there.

My legs were tired but I started jogging. I ran past Five Star, the pizzeria, and by the time I reached the parking lot, my lungs were really whistling. I'd been smoking so much lately that I couldn't catch my breath, but I didn't stop. Getting to the church was the only thing I was sure about.

Weaving my way past couples, I reached the staircase and leapt up the stairs, three at a time. My undershirt was soaked through, both my shoelaces were untied, and I was hyperventilating so loudly that people were staring at me. Another train was waiting in the station and I jumped on the first car. Trudging down the aisle, I fell onto an empty bench. My whole body was sore and I still couldn't breathe, but I was on my way.

———

Danny stood on the corner of 110th and Broadway with his hands nervously stuffed in his pockets. All around him, college kids were lining up for Max's hot dogs and papaya drinks, and I realized I hadn't eaten anything all day.

I walked up behind Danny and put my arm around his shoulders. "You ready?" His body flinched, but he smiled when he realized it was me.

"No," he said, raising his voice. "I'm glad you're here. I wasn't sure—"

"This isn't about Kris and me," I interrupted. I could see that he didn't believe me, but I didn't care. At some point during the train ride, I'd given up trying to piece everything together. It hurt too much. It was easier just to concentrate on the one thing I was sure of—Danny needed my help.

"Either way. I'm still really glad you made it," Danny said. "I owe you for this."

"We'll see how much good it does you."

"You haven't heard from Greg?" Danny asked.

"No, but it's just three-thirty."

"I'm pretty freaked out, Nick."

"I know," I began. "But there's no point in stressing now."

Danny nodded. "You're right. I spent the train ride reading this Army poster," he said, smiling. "I was thinking about joining up. Nobody would find me there."

"Maybe I'll go with you." It was good to see his sense of humor was still in working order. "I could use the exercise. Why don't we join the Navy instead? No one's going to track us down halfway across the Pacific."

"I don't like those pants. We could join the Air Force."

"Nah. You can't wear glasses in the Air Force," I said, putting my finger against my frames. "At least I don't think so."

"How about the Marines?" Danny asked. "We'd get swords."

"Do they ever fight with those things?"

"I don't know."

"Neither do I."

"Well, if this doesn't work out, at least we've got a backup plan," Danny declared, surveying the avenue.

I noticed a tall guy in a Tommy jacket crossing 110th Street. We made eye contact, and he walked over to us. "One of you Thet?" he asked, playing with the drawstring on his jacket.

"Yeah."

"My name's Jason." We shook hands. "Greg just paged me. He wants you guys to head over."

I turned to Danny. "Well, let's go."

"Yo, not to be whack and shit," Jason said, "but I used to really admire your pieces. I mean, when I first started writing."

"I was just copying other people," I said, trying to deflect him. "You know how it is." The compliment was nice, but I was starting to feel like an antique.

Jason nodded and walked over to a newsstand on the corner. "Peace."

Danny and I headed uptown. We passed a pizzeria filled with screaming kids playing arcade games and a lonely take-out Chinese restaurant. The sun was starting to set across the river and, as we crossed each street, I could see the light filtering through the trees in Riverside Park. I couldn't help remembering how Kris and I used to hang out in the playgrounds that lined the entrances to the park.

"I'm getting so fucking sick of prep-school hoods," Danny said.

"You have no idea," I muttered.

"It's so transparent. Look at them." Danny pointed across the street at three hoods standing outside a bodega. Two of the guys were laughing and joking around, and the third was leaning up against a phone booth with his girlfriend wrapped around him. The purple hood of his North Face jacket hid his eyes.

I reached into my pocket and pulled out a set of the brass knuckles. "You ever use these?" I asked, handing them to Danny.

He frowned at me. "The closest I've ever come to throwing a punch is reading Hemingway."

"Well, they're pretty self-explanatory," I said. "I've never used them either, but it's always better to be prepared."

Danny pounded his metal fist into his palm. "Now I just need to learn how to punch."

We headed east and the church started to come into sight. The side streets were darkening and the early-evening dew smelled like wet dirt.

Trinity Church was a small building on the corner of Morningside Drive. The front was decorated with four Corinthian pillars and three tall black doors. There was an old metal gate surrounding the property and encasing a tiny garden that had seen better days. I'd taken a class trip to it years ago, but I hadn't been back since.

The inside of the church was lit with altars scattered with dollar candles. Stained-glass windows lined the sides, but it was too late in the day to really see them. Above, flying buttresses stretched upward into the black.

Greg was sitting in the last row of the pews with his arms stretched out on the back of a wooden bench. There were only five other people in the church. Three old ladies cleaning the altar and a couple praying on the side. I wished there were more people around.

Greg walked over to us and gave me a condescending smile. "How you boyz doing?"

"Where is everybody?" I asked.

"They're here," Greg said, motioning behind his shoulder. "But I figured it'd be best if I met you first."

Greg pulled a porcelain bowl out of his pocket and stuffed it with a pinch. Taking a long hit off his Zippo, he offered the bowl to us. I shook my head. Danny threw me an anxious look, but I couldn't decide if Greg was more or less helpful stoned.

Greg stared up at the ceiling and the floral moldings, and then over at Danny. "God, this place is mad beautiful."

"How many of them are there?" I asked. I wanted to know what we were walking into.

"Three," Greg said angrily. "I told Derrick to bring one other guy, but he was probably nervous. Fucking pussy."

"How many guys did you bring?" Danny asked.

"Only me and Eddie. But that's fine. They figure you two are with me, so it all evens out." Greg took another short hit off his bowl. He lived for shit like this. It justified everything Greg stood for.

"All right, let's do it, Thet. Old-school style," Greg said, turning around and starting down the center aisle.

"Old school," I said, winking at Danny. Greg was so full of shit. We never pulled stunts like this when we were writing together.

Halfway down the aisle, Greg made a right and a group of four guys came into sight. Derrick smiled as soon as he saw me and nudged the guy next to him. Derrick was an ugly fucking kid.

Another one of the guys was leaning up against a church pillar and listening to a mini-disc player. He was wearing a puffy coat that camouflaged his small frame and baggy Levi's. Greg motioned him over.

"This is Eddie," Greg said. "He's with me."

MKII watched the introductions and then walked slowly over to us. Derrick led, and the other two followed closely behind.

"Derrick," Greg said, looking back at us. "Meet Thet and Danny."

"Yeah," Derrick said, grinning. "I met this crazy perv last night."

Greg looked around the circle for an explanation. "Danny's the guy," he said. "And he's here to settle this so that there doesn't have to be any bullshit."

I heard something behind me and turned around. About twenty feet behind us were the three hoods we'd seen standing outside the bodega—we were trapped. The guy wearing the purple North Face lifted his hand to his waist and gave me a short, obnoxious wave, and his girlfriend sat down in the pews and put her feet up. I didn't know what to do.

Eddie leaned toward Greg. "There's too many of them," he said, underneath his breath.

"It's okay," Greg whispered. "Jason saw them on the way in."

"There isn't enough time," Eddie said, his voice getting louder.

"Keep quiet," Greg muttered, giving a mock smile to Derrick.

I looked over at Danny and noticed his leg was shaking. He knew he was fucked.

"Hey, Derrick," Greg began, "I thought this was supposed to be friendly. If I didn't know better—"

"What?" Derrick interrupted.

"Well, I'd think you were starting something."

"And?" Derrick laughed.

"Hell, Derrick, I thought we were friends."

"Yeah, well, friends shouldn't go screwing around with my bitch."

I reached into my back pocket and slid my right hand into the rings of the brass knuckles. My face was sweating and my pulse was drumming against my ears. Drawing my fist to my side, I clenched my fingers and felt the metal draw heat.

Greg turned to Eddie and shook his head. "What a fucking mess. We're here to apologize."

"I don't want a fucking apology," Derrick said, taking a step toward Greg.

Across the aisle, the middle-aged couple saw what was happening and started walking quickly toward the exit.

"Derrick, if you start this," Greg said calmly, "I mean, if your bitch ass starts this, you better fucking kill me. Because if you don't, I will track you down and beat the living shit out of you."

Derrick took another step toward Greg. I could hear the footsteps of the hoods behind us; then there was a pause and everything went into slow motion. It couldn't have lasted more than a second, but we all shared it. Then Eddie tried to step between Derrick and Greg, and it all began. Derrick's two friends grabbed Greg and threw him against a stone pillar. Greg's jacket cushioned the blow, but his head slammed into the limestone.

The three hoods from the bodega jumped Danny and Eddie, and Derrick started for me. Our eyes met; Derrick nodded confidently. He leaned back to swing with his right and then jabbed with his left. Ducking to the side, I threw a right into his stomach. The brass was off and slammed into his hipbone. Derrick gasped—the metal recoil sliced into my knuckles. I couldn't believe I fucking hit him. I swung wildly again at Derrick's face and missed. He shoved me back, and I fell into a wooden pew.

"I'm gonna fuck you up, bitch," Derrick yelled.

Scrambling to my feet, I backed down the aisle away from Derrick. He reached into his jacket, and over his shoulder I could see Danny being held up against a pillar. Flipping out a butterfly knife, Derrick twirled the blades with his wrist. He leapt toward me, and I jumped back. Derrick lunged for me again and walked into my left fist. The punch nailed him across the jaw and I felt something give in his mouth as I followed through. I didn't know what I was doing, but it was working. I threw a right into Derrick's eye, dropped him against the pew, and kicked the butterfly knife out of his hand. Stepping on his chest, I took off down the aisle for Danny.

Two hoods still had Danny pressed against the pillar. Danny's nose was bleeding down his shirt and I could see his right eye starting to swell. I had so much foot speed by the time I reached them that I dived onto one of the hoods. The collision knocked us both to the ground, and I threw my fist into his nose as we fell. I started to swing again and suddenly it was as if every candle in the church had blown out. My chin hit the marble floor, and my teeth slammed shut. Sirens were screaming. I opened my eyes for a second, and from the ground all I could see was the silhouette of a dozen guys standing just inside Trinity Church.

———

I couldn't see anything. I was sitting down, and my neck and back were hunched forward. Someone's arm was pressed against my stomach, holding my chest up, and my head was killing me. I reached up with my hand to see if I was bleeding. My glasses were gone.

"Don't say a word, Cowboy."

I was dizzy, nauseous. "Kris?"

"Ssshh."

"Where are you?" I whispered.

"I'm right next to you." Her cheek brushed against my shoulder, and I realized I was sitting on her lap. I knew I was woozy but I still loved the sound of her voice, tickling my ears.

"Why can't I see anything?"

"Ssshh."

I felt like going back to sleep. "Where is everybody?"

"Quiet."

"Where's Danny?"

Kris's fingertips ran down my nose and pressed my lips together. "Stay quiet."

I nodded, and felt the back of my neck rub against her chin.

Suddenly, I could hear people talking, but I didn't recognize any of the voices. And then it faded.

"Kris," I began. "Where are we?"

"Look to your right."

I turned my head, and the muscles and joints in my neck seemed to cry out in unison. Six inches from my face were a dozen pin-sized holes in the shape of a diamond. Tiny streams of light were pouring through the holes and illuminating the dust floating in the air. For a second, I thought we were in a coffin but I was almost positive we weren't lying down.

Twisting back toward Kris, I saw the checkered pattern of light resting on her sleeve. I raised my head a couple of inches and through the holes I could see the outlines of two cops.

"Cops?" I said, running my hand over my head again and searching for the source of the dull ache. I still didn't know where I was, but I was happy staying put.

I felt Kris nod.

"Where's Danny?"

"Arrested." Kris sighed.

"Greg?"

"Arrested."

"Where are we?" I muttered.

"In the confessional."

I let out a small laugh and Kris tightened her hold around my stomach. "Sorry," I said, still grinning. "How'd we get in here?"

"I dragged you."

"By yourself?" I said, surprised.

Kris nodded again.

"How long have we been in here?"

"Half an hour."

"Why?"

"Because the cops were coming," she said.

I tried to remember the fight, but I couldn't picture Kris anywhere. "Where'd you come from?"

"I called Tracy before I got home," she whispered. "She overheard some MKIIs talking about this meeting and ambushing the Diggs. I tried to get here in time to warn Danny."

Through the holes in the confessional, I could see the two cops getting smaller. "They're leaving," I mumbled.

"You sure?"

I pressed my face against the openings. "Yup."

"All right, then let's get out of here. Okay?"

I didn't want to stand up, but it was easier just to nod.

"When I open the door," Kris continued. "Just follow me outside. Okay?"

"Okay."

"Here are your glasses," she said, placing the frames in my palm. "One of the lenses got knocked out when you got hit. It's in my pocket."

I slid my glasses back on. They were bent out of shape, and it made me smile. In the movies, the guy's glasses are always crooked after the fight.

"Can you see?" Kris asked.

"I don't know."

"Can you walk?"

"I hope so," I said.

Kris leaned to her right and a wave of light poured in. My eyes hurt, but now I could see the frame of the confessional. She pushed the door open halfway and lifted me up. My legs felt limp, but they seemed to hold me.

"Now walk," Kris said, leading me out.

A cop was down near the altar, but he had his back to us. Kris wrapped her arm around my waist and walked me slowly toward the street. It was dark outside, and the streetlights on Morningside were on. I could only see through my left eye, but I spotted the empty cop car.

"Don't stop," Kris said.

She helped me down the steps and onto the pavement, and then we walked along Morningside. I don't know why, but it was as if every different feeling I'd ever had was pushing its way to the surface. I was proud that I'd showed up for Danny, but I still felt like a failure.

"You've got to get to a hospital," Kris said. "You're going to need stitches."

"I think so," I said, feeling the dried blood in my hair. "Can we sit down for a minute?"

We crossed 110th Street and sat on the steps of a brownstone.

Kris rested her head in her hands. "I can't believe what they did to my brother." When she sat up, I saw two tears slide down her cheekbone and dissolve into her hair.

"What happened? I can't really remember," I said, fighting another wave of nausea. It was easier not to talk.

"When I showed up, everybody was fighting. You dove onto these kids, and then this girl hit you over the head with one of those blackjack things. You went down fast, Nick."

"But I thought I saw more people," I said, confused. "Were those cops?"

"No, they were Dignitaries. They beat the shit out of everybody," Kris said disgustedly. "Even the girl. Then the cops showed up, and everybody scattered."

"They arrested Danny?"

"Yeah. He was still fighting, or trying to fight." Kris took a deep breath and leaned back against the steps. "He was surrounded, so I dragged you into the confessional. I didn't want you getting arrested, too."

"Is he gonna be okay?" I wished I could have pulled that other guy off of him.

"I don't know. His right eye looked pretty messed up," Kris said. "But he wasn't as bad as that kid in the purple jacket. The medics had to bring him out on a gurney."

Kris shook her head angrily. "Here's your lens." She pulled it out of her pocket and handed it to me. "Let's get you in a cab," she said, helping me up. "I'll call my mother from the hospital. I need to get over to the police station to check on Danny."

Kris hailed a taxi on 110th and opened the door for me. "St. Luke's ER," she told the driver.

The cabbie looked nervously over at me, and I faked a grin. "I'm pregnant," I said.

Kris placed her arm around my hunched shoulders. "Rest your head on me."

"I don't want to bleed on you."

"It's okay," Kris said, pulling me toward her.

I laid my forehead against her sweater and closed my eyes. After the last forty-eight hours with Kris, I couldn't decide what to think or say or do. I just needed to rest.

Lying in a hospital bed, it's amazing how many different shapes you can make out in plastic ceiling tiles. I knew the painkillers were riding their way through my veins, because I kept smiling at the floral posters on the walls.

When Kris had walked me into the ER, the doctors had shaved a silver dollar–sized section above my right ear, stitched me back up, and wrapped my forehead in gauze. Now the only things that still really hurt were my hands. The skin was carved away from my pinkie knuckle, and I could see dry bone when I flexed. I kept guessing which punches were responsible.

The gray curtains around my bed parted, and my mother's worried face peered in. She wasn't wearing any makeup, and I wondered if the doctors had woken her up in the middle of the night, or even if it was the middle of the night.

"How are you feeling?" my mother asked, sitting down on the side of my bed. She leaned toward me and pressed the back of her hand to my damp forehead.

"I'm wonderful," I said. I raised my pillow and felt a chorus of aches.

Elliot trailed behind my mother and dropped his fedora at the foot of my blanket. I didn't feel like dealing with him, but I couldn't walk out on them this time.

Elliot's eyes moved their way up from my untied shoelace to my ripped jeans to my bruised cheekbone. "You seem to be starting fights everywhere you go."

My mother shook her head slowly and pulled out a small packet of tissues. I couldn't tell whether she was annoyed by my bruises or Elliot's tone of voice.

"Nick," he began. "I know my teenage years were different from yours, both because I was at Exmoor and because of the times, but there have to be more constructive things to do."

"I'm sorry," I mumbled, not making eye contact. I was too out of it to start arguing with the guy.

My mother rested her hand on my shoulder. A tear formed in the corner of her eye, slid down her cheek, and then disappeared between her lips. I hadn't seen her cry since she married Elliot. I guessed that she did, but never in front of me, never about me. It felt really strange. I guess it felt good.

"Elliot," my mother said. "He's hurt."

"I—" I started.

"Not by accident," Elliot said. "That's—"

"He's hurt," my mother declared. She lifted my left hand and studied the damage. "With your head wrapped up," she whispered, "you look just like your dad used to. You guys both have a knack for ending up in hospitals."

"I didn't want to fight," I said. "I swear."

"What am I supposed to do with you?" She sighed. "I'm totally at a loss."

Elliot opened the drapes in my room and checked on the windowsill for dust. It was dark outside. "Ground him. For starters." If I'd had the energy, I would've told him to go fuck himself.

"Get some more sleep," my mother said, kissing my cheek. "Your doctor says that's the most important thing right now."

They walked out into the hallway and I went back to staring at ceiling tiles. When Kodak went down, I'd spent half the night in the refreshment room wishing I could trade places with him. I'd even thought about going into the bathroom and smashing my fist into the sink mirror, just so I'd have a scrape or cut or bruise. But lying there now, wrapped up like a Christmas gift, I didn't know what to think.

The curtain swung open, and Danny appeared holding a suitcase. His right eye was blanketed with a square sheet of gauze, and his upper lip was deep violet.

"You awake or sleeping?" Danny asked.

"I'm too stoned to do either," I said, trying to roll onto my side and failing. It was good to see him. "I thought you were in jail."

"My sister begged them not to hold me. Eventually, they released Daniel H. Conway on his own recognizance, with a court date and everything," he said, picking up a container of Percocet on my nightstand. He twirled the top off and pulled out a white capsule. "Can you believe they leave shit like this out?"

"Put it back," I muttered.

Danny sat down at the foot of my bedspread. "Hell no." Unzipping his suitcase, he slipped the container inside his bag. "This makes the whole fucking weekend worthwhile."

"How you doing?" I asked, gesturing toward his face.

"Been better." I could hear a soft lisp in his voice from all the swelling. "It's funny, but the first punch is the only one that really hurt. You know." He pressed his palm against his ribcage and winced. "What's that line, 'After the first punch, there is no other.'"

"Something like that," I said, grinning.

"Well, I'm getting the hell out of Dodge." Danny stood up. "And I wanted to invite you."

"Where?"

Danny winked with his one good eye. "California. What do you say?"

I was too tired to breathe, and he wanted me to go to California. "Why?"

"Come on." He stretched his arms wide and raised his palms to the ceiling. "*On the Road,* Jack and Neal making a run of it."

"You can't drive."

"I know. But my father's picking me up at the airport."

I laughed and felt a crisp pinch in my lungs. "Why so soon?"

"Nick," Danny said, raising his eyebrows in disbelief, "we're marked men. Greg spent an hour in the holding tank explaining to me how the Diggs are gonna massacre MKII. He's already prepping for your initiation ceremony."

"Tell him we're Conformists," I declared. Couldn't Greg wait until I was out of the fucking hospital?

Danny nodded. "I tried. He's not the smartest kid, you know."

Kris pushed aside the curtain and fell into the plastic chair at my bedside. She rolled her eyes at her brother. "He's not going with you," she said, placing a brown paper bag on my nightstand.

"Let the man decide for himself," Danny said.

"I'm cool," I said. I couldn't understand how Kris seemed so relaxed around me.

"Your loss." Danny reached out his hand to shake, and I noticed a metal splint binding his first two fingers together. We held hands for a second, and then he lifted his suitcase to his side. "Thanks, Nick," Danny said, tipping an imaginary hat.

"No problem." I didn't want him to leave. I was getting used to Danny's endless philosophies. "When are you coming back?"

"When everything cools off." Kris walked over to Danny, gave him a kiss on the cheek, and then pulled him into a gentle hug. "Or in time for the court date."

Danny looked back at me and grinned. "We could have a lot of—"

"Get going," Kris said, fighting a smile.

Danny waved good-bye behind his back and disappeared into the maze of curtains. Even after I lost sight of him, I could hear hundreds of little capsules rattling in his suitcase.

"Your mother wants him out of the city?" I asked, trying to fill the silence.

Kris sat back down and reached into the paper bag. "Yeah, she called my dad from the precinct. They decided to put him on a flight ASAP." She pulled out two cups of coffee. "I couldn't figure out what else to buy you," she said, passing me a cup. "Regular, right?"

"Thanks," I said, surprised. "You know, you don't have to stay here." I didn't want her pity.

"I've got no better place to be."

"What about with Luke?" I had to ask, even though it stung.

"It's just really complicated."

"Huh." The warm coffee traced the soreness in my chest and ribs and stomach. "It sounded pretty simple earlier."

"Nick . . ." Kris hesitated. "I want to thank you." She sat forward in her chair and rubbed my leg through the blanket. "I mean, I'll always owe you for helping him."

I looked down at my sheets. "I didn't do it for you."

"I know. That's part of the reason it means so much to me." Kris stood up from her chair and sat on the side of my bed. She pressed her hand softly against my hip. "Slide over," she said, smiling.

I handed her my cup of coffee, lifted myself up on my arms,

and moved to the edge of the mattress. Kris adjusted my spare pillow and lay down next to me. I loved having her by my side again, but it scared the shit out of me. Couldn't she see how broken I was after this morning?

"You know," Kris said. "I've never been so confused in my entire life."

"How do you mean?" Was she trying to torture me?

"I've just spent the last twenty-four hours trying to sort everything out, the difference between friendship and love and . . ." Her voice trailed off. "It's impossible."

"If it makes you feel any better," I began, "I haven't been able to tell the difference for a while now."

"But you know what you want, right?"

"Yeah," I said, staring out the window. I didn't have the strength to look her in the eyes. "As much as I know anything."

Kris turned to face me. "Can you give me some time?"

Before I could figure out what to say, I realized I was nodding. "But what do we do until you figure everything out?"

She shrugged. "I guess you'll have to keep waking me up in the middle of the night."

"Sometimes I don't know who else I can talk to," I confessed.

"Well, you're lucky you don't have to."

I rolled onto my side and lay my head on Kris's shoulder. I'd run out of words and explanations and arguments. "No matter what, you make an incredible pillow."

She slid her shoes off against the bedside railing and covered her legs with my blanket. "You know what I was watching in the waiting room?"

"What?" I said, studying the pale arch of her neck.

"*The Wizard of Oz.* I thought you'd be proud of me, Cowboy."

"I am."

"Well, have you ever noticed how important Toto is?" she asked, lifting my forearm and gently squeezing it.

"Toto?" I mumbled.

"Yeah, Toto. Okay, when the movie starts out, what's going on?"

I rested my palm on her hipbone. "It's black-and-white."

"Toto's the reason Dorothy is so upset and decides to run away."

"Because that old bag is trying to kill him." I had no idea why we were debating *The Wizard of Oz,* but it felt good just to talk.

"Exactly," she said, carefully rubbing my wrist. "But Toto escapes from the basket."

"I still think it's Dorothy's story." I pulled the blanket to my collar and curled my legs toward Kris. "Toto's just a plot point."

"Or look at the ending. Toto and Dorothy are captured by the flying monkeys. Do you remember how they're saved?"

"I barely remember my middle name right now."

Kris smiled. "They're saved because Toto escapes from the witch's castle and goes and finds the three guys. Same with the ending. Toto's the one who discovers the Wizard is just some sleazy old man."

I felt my toes press against Kris's ankle. "Maybe they should have called the movie *Toto.*"

"I'm being serious." Kris laughed and massaged the back of my neck. "When I was younger, I was so obsessed with Dorothy that I never realized how important the little guy is."

"Judy Garland was your idol?" I said, yawning.

"Oh, come on." She looked over at me. "Everyone has a hero. Little kids are just the only ones smart enough to admit it."

I closed my eyes and let my lips brush softly against her sweater. "You should go home and get some sleep."

"I'll stay," Kris whispered.

Monday

My eyes slid open and I squinted at the fluorescent hospital bulbs. I stretched my back and yawned at the wool curtains. Outside my window, the bricks were soaked in a warm turquoise light. I figured it was dawn, but it might be dusk.

I turned to my right and smiled when I saw Kris. She was draped in a pair of lime-green blankets and snoring softly against the metal frame of my bedside chair. This was the second morning I'd woken up next to her, but this time I was sure that she cared about me.

Sitting up in bed, I tossed the sheets to the side. They'd changed me into a gray hospital gown, and I scanned the room for my clothes. I couldn't find my hoodie. I rolled off the mattress, my feet falling quietly onto the cool linoleum, and reached for my jeans and Timberlands. My kneecaps were still swollen, but I slid the jeans back on and lifted my backpack onto my shoulders.

I walked over to Kris and placed my hand gently on her arm. "I'll be back in a few," I whispered. She nodded faintly, and I tucked the blankets against her body. I was never going to get used to how beautiful she was.

I leaned out into the hallway and checked the floor for doctors. I wasn't sure if they'd let me leave and I didn't want to chance it. There were a couple of nurses at the far end of the floor flipping through clipboards. I stepped into the hallway and walked as quickly as I could in the other direction. I felt like Jack Nicholson in *One Flew Over the Cuckoo's Nest,* but nobody else in the ward was around to cheer me on.

After about fifty paces, I found an empty elevator bank and pressed the down arrow. The doors slid open a few seconds later, and two nurses surveyed my hospital gown—I was fucked. Stepping in between them, I searched the panel of buttons. There was an *L,* an *M,* and three different-number *P*s. I had no clue what to push, so I hit *L.*

"Can I help you?" the taller nurse asked, leaning toward me.

"Just going outside for a butt," I said, waiting for one of them to jab a needle in my arm.

"A lot of people quit while they're in the hospital," the other nurse said.

I shrugged as casually as I could.

On the third floor, the elevator doors slid open again and the nurses stepped off. I'd made it.

Back on Amsterdam, I spotted a taxi waiting for the light to change. I slid across the vinyl seat and asked the driver to take me to 22nd and Sixth. My forehead was still aching, but it felt good to be out of the hospital. I just couldn't remember if the piece was off Sixth or Fifth. The night Kodak and I put it up, we were drinking Crazy Horse like it was going out of style, and I hadn't been back to the wall in at least a year. I knew the piece was still up, though, because Jerry had asked me about it a couple of weeks ago. It was my last one.

The taxi sailed down Ninth, and I studied the fresh scabs on my fingers. The clock in the cab read 5:02 A.M. Kris was probably still asleep, curled up in her chair. I had no idea what she'd think if she woke up, but I knew I'd be able to explain it to her later.

When the cabbie turned onto 22nd, I asked him to drive slowly down the street. I knew I'd recognize the parking lot. Kodak and I had spent four hours there standing on the roof of a minivan. Halfway toward Fifth, I spotted my jagged lettering. I handed the driver a five and grabbed my backpack off the seat.

Two years later, the piece was still strong. It started ten feet up the parking lot wall, and the three gray-blue characters were taller than I was. Writers had plastered the brick below with tags and blockbusters, but my wildstyles had hung in there.

Surveying the block, I spotted a pay phone outside a shuttered sports bar. I pushed a quarter into the coin slot, leaned against the inside of the booth, and dialed Greg's cell. I hoped he wasn't still in the holding tank.

After the second ring, I started practicing my message. "Hey, it's Nick . . ." "'Morning, it's . . ."

"S'up," Greg said.

I straightened up, startled. "It's Nick."

"Thet," he shouted. "Wassup, kid? How you feeling, yo?"

"Not bad. The cops hold you?"

"Hell, no." Greg laughed. "My pops sent his lawyer."

"Where are you?"

"Chilling at Jason's crib, working on the MKII plan. Shit's gonna be like the fucking crusades."

"Hey, I need you to meet me at the Twenty-second Street wall," I said. "You know, where my piece is."

"Oh shit. Thet's back," he howled. "But I don't have cans."

"Don't worry about it. I've got'm for both of us."

"I'll be there in twenty. And get back to work, homes. We gots years to make up for." *Beep.*

I hung up the phone and started walking back to the lot. Across the block, two busboys were hosing down the sidewalk outside an Italian restaurant. A bread truck was idling in the alleyway next to the restaurant, and I felt like asking the busboys for a bagel or roll or something.

A red Explorer was parked underneath my piece, and I climbed the chrome bumper. Pushing myself onto the roof of the car, I threw my legs over and planted them against a ski rack. I stood up on top of the Explorer and unzipped my backpack. Reaching into my bag, I flipped off the cap on a can of Krylon Black.

I stared at my lettering and took a full breath. I still loved the blends and highlights. I couldn't believe I was about to cross myself out. Had anyone ever done this before?

Raising my arm to the clouds, I sprayed long black streaks down the surface of the brick. Thick streams of paint washed away the silvers and blues, and my *A* dissolved into a tiny triangle. Flexing my wrist back and forth, I mixed the can again and then leaned into the wall. My *O* collapsed into a broken *C* and I waved my arm across the width of the piece. Misting Krylon started to settle on my fingertips and nails. Halfway through my *D,* I remembered the way Kodak had spent ten minutes detailing the shinemarks on the arch, and then it was gone. Puddles of paint started to grip the brick, but I didn't let up on that cap. It felt too good to stop.

After a few minutes, the can sputtered and deflated. I tossed the empty into my backpack and sat down on the roof of the Explorer. I pulled out my pack of cigarettes and searched for a match. Taking a soft drag, I smiled at the shining black rectangle. It looked like someone had painted a floating doorway fifteen feet in the air.

The first thing I heard was Greg's voice. "What the fuck is that?"

I looked up and saw Greg walking across 22nd Street. He was wearing a loose Polo jumpsuit and pointing a half-eaten bagel.

"'Morning," I said, hopping down from the Explorer. A set of brass knuckles had left a cookie-cutter bruise on his cheek.

"Yo, why'd you roll your piece?"

"I'm retiring," I began. "Retiring Thet for good."

"Fuck you retiring." Greg laughed and took another bite. "You must've had one of those crazy laptopomies or whatever," he said, staring at my bandaged head.

"No, for real."

"Thet, chillz. What the fuck are you even talking about, kid?"

"Me." I don't know why, but I wasn't afraid of Greg. I was exhausted and sore and confused, but I wasn't afraid. "I'm done. With *DOA,* with Thet."

Greg shook his head disgustedly. "So your punk ass crossed yourself out?" I nodded and he pointed angrily at the wall. "And what do you think that shit means?"

"It was my last piece," I declared.

"Nah," he sneered. "What do you think that shit means to me? Your bitch ass still owes me for throwing down at the church."

"I didn't want you to fight." My voice was firm. "I didn't want anybody to fight."

Greg sidearmed the rest of his bagel into a dumpster. "You still owe me."

"What do you want me to do?"

He smiled. "Roll with me on this mission we're planning."

"I can't."

"Fine. Once your head's healed."

"No," I said calmly.

"Your shit's a one-way street," he exploded.

"I'm just not about violence or street cred or any of it." I reached into my pocket and found Ella wrapped up in a couple bills. It felt good to have him with me on this one.

"And when Derrick comes after you?" Greg smirked.

Derrick had the Diggs to deal with first. MKII would come for me eventually, but there was no changing that now. "I'll think of something."

Greg wrapped his hands behind his head. "So your punk ass thinks you can just walk away from everything?"

"I'm doing it."

"What if I say you're not?" Greg asked.

"Let it be over."

He scanned the avenue and laughed. "You're such a pussy, Nick. You know that?"

I shrugged it off. "We're just different guys."

"You gotta quit hiding from your past, kid."

"I'm not," I said, wondering if it were true.

"Well, you could've fooled me." Greg pulled out his vibrating Nokia and lifted it to his ear. "Jason, shit's on for six in the evening, okay. . . . Nah, his head's too cut up," he said, glaring at me. "Okay. . . . Peace." Greg slapped the cell shut. "I gotta bust."

"All right."

We started walking toward Fifth. Up the block, two suits were loading the trunk of a Lincoln with their carry-ons.

"They landed one good one on you?" I asked, pointing at his cheek.

"Lucky first jab," Greg said. "Wassup with your head?"

"Stitches. That girl blackjacked me from behind."

"Fucking savages," he declared. "They deserve this crazy ambush we're cooking."

A taxi pulled up to the red light on 22nd, and Greg raised hi arm to hail it.

"See you around," I said, reaching out my hand.

He smiled. "I'll never figure you out, kid." We shook hands and he swung the cab door open.

The light clicked back to green, and the cab turned onto Fifth. I stood on the corner, watching Greg's taxi drift down the avenue.

I stretched my arms in the air and searched Fifth for a deli or diner. I felt like walking back to the hospital, and I needed something to keep me going. Kris might be asleep, but she was waiting for me.